Leo Tolstoy was born in central Russia in 1828. He studied Oriental languages and law (though failed to earn a degree in the latter) at the University of Kazan, and after a dissolute youth eventually joined an artillery regiment in the Caucusus in 1851. He took part in the Crimean War, and the *Sebastopol Sketches* that emerged from it established his reputation. After living for some time in St Petersburg and abroad, he married Sophie Behrs in 1862 and they had thirteen children. The happiness this brought him gave him the creative impulse for his two greatest novels, *War and Peace* (1869) and *Anna Karenina* (1877). Later in life his views became increasingly radical as he gave up his possessions in order to live a simple peasant life. After a quarrel with his wife he fled home secretly one night to seek refuge in a monastery. He became ill and died during this dramatic flight, at the small railway station of Astapovo, in 1910.

LEO TOLSTOY

The Death of
Ivan Ilyich

Translated by Anthony Briggs

PENGUIN BOOKS

PENGUIN BOOKS

Published by the Penguin Group
Penguin Books Ltd, 80 Strand, London WC2R ORL, England
Penguin Group (USA) Inc., 375 Hudson Street, New York, New York 10014, USA
Penguin Group (Canada), 90 Eglinton Avenue East, Suite 700,
Toronto, Ontario, Canada M4P 2Y3 (a division of Pearson Penguin Canada Inc.)
Penguin Ireland, 25 St Stephen's Green, Dublin 2, Ireland
(a division of Penguin Books Ltd)
Penguin Group (Australia), 250 Camberwell Road, Camberwell, Victoria 3124,
Australia (a division of Pearson Australia Group Pty Ltd)
Penguin Books India Pvt Ltd, 11 Community Centre,
Panchsheel Park, New Delhi – 110 017, India
Penguin Group (NZ), cnr Airborne and Rosedale Roads, Albany,
Auckland 1310, New Zealand (a division of Pearson New Zealand Ltd)
Penguin Books (South Africa) (Pty) Ltd, 24 Sturdee Avenue,
Rosebank, Johannesburg 2196, South Africa

Penguin Books Ltd, Registered Offices: 80 Strand, London WC2R ORL, England

www.penguin.com

First published in Russian in 1886
Published as a Penguin Red Classic 2006

1

Copyright © Anthony Briggs, 2006

Set in MT Dante
Typeset by Palimpsest Book Production Limited, Polmont, Stirlingshire
Printed in England by Clays Ltd, St Ives plc

Except in the United States of America, this book is sold subject
to the condition that it shall not, by way of trade or otherwise, be lent,
re-sold, hired out, or otherwise circulated without the publisher's
prior consent in any form of binding or cover other than that in
which it is published and without a similar condition including this
condition being imposed on the subsequent purchaser

ISBN-13: 978-0-14102-360-1
ISBN-10: 0-14102-360-0

I

In the large Law Court building, during an adjournment of the Melvinsky trial, the members of the bench and the Public Prosecutor had come together in the office of Ivan Yegorovich Shebek, and the conversation touched on the celebrated Krasovsky case. Fyodor Vasilyevich argued vehemently that it was beyond their jurisdiction, Ivan Yegorovich had his own view and was sticking to it, while Pyotr Ivanovich, who had kept out of the discussion at the outset and was still not contributing, was perusing a copy of *The Gazette* which had just been delivered.

'Gentlemen!' he said. 'Ivan Ilyich is dead.'

'Is he really?'

'Here you are. Read it yourself,' he said to Fyodor Vasilyevich, handing him the paper, fresh off the press and still smelling.

There was an announcement within a black border: 'It is with profound sorrow that Praskovya Fyodorovna Golovina informs family and friends that her beloved husband, Ivan Ilyich Golovin, Member of the Court of Justice, passed away on the 4th of February this year, 1882. The funeral will take place on Friday at 1 p.m.'

Ivan Ilyich had been a colleague of the gentlemen

assembled there, and they had all liked him. He had been ill for several weeks, and the word was that his illness was incurable. His post had been kept open for him, but there was an understanding that in the event of his death Alexeyev would step into his place, and Alexeyev's place would be taken by either Vinnikov or Shtabel. So, the first thought that occurred to each of the assembled gentlemen on hearing the news of his death was how this death might affect his own prospects, and those of their acquaintances, for transfer or promotion.

'I'm sure to get Shtabel's job now, or Vinnikov's,' thought Fyodor Vasilyevich. 'They promised me ages ago, and a promotion like that would give me another eight hundred roubles a year, plus expenses.'

'I must apply to have my brother-in-law transferred from Kaluga,' thought Pyotr Ivanovich. 'My wife will be delighted. She won't be able to tell me I never do anything for her people.'

'I had a feeling he wasn't going to get better,' said Pyotr Ivanovich. 'It's sad.'

'What was actually wrong with him?'

'The doctors couldn't decide. Well, they could, but they all decided differently. The last time I saw him I thought he was going to come through it.'

'And I hadn't been to see him since Christmas. I kept meaning to go.'

'Was he all right financially?'

'His wife had a bit of money, I think. Nothing very much.'

'Well, we'll have to go and see her. They live an awfully long way away.'

'For you they do. Where you live, everywhere's a long way away.'

'Look at that. He can't forgive me for living across the river,' said Pyotr Ivanovich, smiling at Shebek. The conversation turned to the long distances between the different parts of the city, and then they walked back into session.

Apart from the speculations aroused in each of them by this death, concerning the transfers and possible changes that this death might bring about, the very fact of the death of someone close to them aroused in all who heard about it, as always, a feeling of delight that he had died and they hadn't.

'There you have it. He's dead, and I'm not' was what everyone thought or felt. But his closest acquaintances, Ivan Ilyich's so-called friends, couldn't help thinking that they would now have to fulfil some tedious social obligations such as attending the funeral and calling on the widow to express their condolences.

Closest of all were Fyodor Vasilyevich and Pyotr Ivanovich.

Pyotr Ivanovich was an old friend from law school, and he felt indebted to Ivan Ilyich.

Over dinner he told his wife about the death of Ivan Ilyich and the mooted possibility of her brother being transferred to their district, and then, dispensing with his usual nap, he put on a dress-coat and set off for Ivan Ilyich's house.

3

At the entrance stood a carriage and two cabs. Downstairs in the entrance hall, next to the coat stand, a coffin lid with silk brocade, tassels and gold braid that had been powdered and polished stood propped against a wall. Two ladies in black were taking off their fur cloaks. He knew one of them, Ivan Ilyich's sister, but not the other. His colleague Schwartz was at the top of the stairs about to come down, but when he saw Pyotr Ivanovich he stopped and gave him a wink that seemed to say, 'Ivan Ilyich has messed things up – not what you or I would have done.'

Schwartz's face with its English side-whiskers and his lean figure in formal dress, exuded, as always, an air of elegant solemnity, and although the solemnity belied his playful personality it was particularly poignant here, or so it seemed to Pyotr Ivanovich.

Pyotr Ivanovich allowed the ladies to pass on ahead, and slowly followed them upstairs. Instead of coming down Schwartz stood waiting at the top. Pyotr Ivanovich knew why; he clearly wanted to arrange a game of whist somewhere that evening. The ladies proceeded upstairs to see the widow, but Schwartz pursed his lips tightly with all seri-ousness, though his eyes had a mischievous look as he twitched his eyebrows, directing Pyotr Ivanovich off to the right and into the room where the dead man lay.

Pyotr Ivanovich entered the room, and hesi-tated, as people always do on these occasions, not knowing precisely what to do. The only thing he was certain of was that in this situation you couldn't go wrong if you made the sign of the cross. Whether or not you should bow at the same time he wasn't sure, so he went for a compromise, crossing himself as he walked in and giving a bit of a bow as he did so. At the same time, as far as hand and head movements permitted, he glanced round the room. Two young persons, nephews apparently, one of them a schoolboy, were crossing themselves as they left the room. A little old woman was standing there motionless. And a lady with curiously arched eyebrows was whispering to her. A Church reader in a frock-coat – a hearty character of considerable spirit – was reading something out in a loud voice and a tone that brooked no contradiction. Gerasim, the peasant who waited at table, darted ahead of Pyotr Ivanovich, sprinkling something on the floor. Seeing this, Pyotr Ivanovich instantly recognized a slight smell of decaying flesh. When he had visited Pyotr Ivanovich for the last time he had seen this peasant in Ivan Ilyich's room, acting as a sick nurse, and Ivan Ilyich had had a special fondness for him.

Pyotr Ivanovich kept on crossing himself, and aimed a slight bow midway between the reader, the coffin and the icons on the corner table. Then, when the business of crossing himself seemed to be going on too long, he paused and took a close look at the dead man.

The dead man lay as all dead men lie, unusually heavy with his dead weight, with rigid limbs sinking into the soft lining of the coffin and his head bowed for eternity on the pillow, and he displayed what dead people always display, a waxen yellow forehead (with bald patches over his hollow temples) and a protruding nose that seemed to be pressing down hard on his upper lip. He had changed a good deal; he was even thinner than he had been when Pyotr Ivanovich had last seen him, but, as with all dead bodies, his face had acquired greater beauty, or, more to the point, greater significance, than it had had in life. Its expression seemed to say that what needed to be done had been done, and done properly. More than that, the expression contained a reproach or at least a reminder to the living. The reminder seemed out of place to Pyotr Ivanovich, or at least he felt it didn't apply to him personally. But an unpleasant feeling came over him, and he crossed himself again, hurriedly – too hurriedly, he thought, the haste was almost indecent – before turning and heading for the door.

Schwartz was waiting for him in the next room with his feet planted wide apart and both hands fiddling with the top-hat held behind his back. One glance at his mischievous, immaculately elegant figure and Pyotr Ivanovich felt restored. He could see that Schwartz was above all this, and would be impervious to anything that might have been depressing. His very appearance spoke volumes: in no way would the occasion of Ivan Ilyich's funeral serve as a reason for cancelling their usual session; in other words nothing would prevent them from breaking open a new pack and riffling through the cards that evening while a servant set up four new candles. There was, in fact, no reason to think that this occasion should stop them having a good time that very evening. He said so in a low voice to Pyotr Ivanovich as he walked past, proposing that they meet for a game at Fyodor Vasilyevich's.

But Pyotr Ivanovich was clearly not destined to play whist that evening. Praskovya Fyodorovna, a short, plump woman whose body expanded from the shoulders down despite her best efforts to the contrary, done out in black, with a lace shawl over her head and the same curiously arched eyebrows as the lady facing the coffin, emerged from her chambers with some other ladies, showed them to the door of the dead man's room, and said, 'The service is about to begin. Do go in.'

Schwartz made an indeterminate bow, and stood there without accepting or rejecting this invitation. Praskovya, recognizing Pyotr Ivanovich, gave a sigh, went straight up to him, took him by the hand and said, 'I know you were a good friend to Ivan Ilyich . . .' And she looked at him, anticipating a suitable response. Pyotr Ivanovich knew that just as he had had to cross himself in there, out here it was necessary to squeeze her hand, and say with a sigh, 'Believe me . . .' And that's what he did. Having done it he felt that the desired effect had been achieved – he had been touched, and she had been touched.

'Let's go in before they get started. I must have a word with you,' said the widow. 'Give me your arm.'

Pyotr Ivanovich offered an arm and they made their way into the inner rooms, walking past Schwartz, who gave Pyotr Ivanovich a gloomy wink. 'No whist for you then. You won't mind if we find another partner. We might make up a five-some when you can get free,' said his mischievous glance.

Pyotr Ivanovich sighed even more deeply and plaintively, and Praskovya showed her gratitude by squeezing his hand. Proceeding into her drawing-room, which was done out in pink cretonne and lit by one dismal lamp, they sat down near to a table, she on a sofa, he on a low pouffe with broken springs that wobbled unevenly as he sat on it. Praskovya had wanted to warn him off into another chair, but a warning like that did not seem appropriate in the circumstances so she thought better of it. As he sat down on his pouffe, Pyotr Ivanovich remembered the time when Ivan Ilyich had been decorating this room and had asked his advice about this pink cretonne with the green leaves. On her way past the table to sit down on the sofa – the room was crammed with furniture and knick-knacks – Praskovya snagged the black lace of her black shawl on the carved edge of the table. Pyotr Ivanovich rose slightly to disentangle it, thus releasing the pouffe, which quivered and pushed up at him. The widow began disentangling the lace herself, so Pyotr Ivanovich sat down again, crushing the rebellious pouffe back into submission. But the widow had not finished disentangling herself, so Pyotr Ivanovich rose again, and so did the pouffe, rebellious and even creaking. When this was all over she took out a clean cambric handkerchief and burst into tears. But Pyotr Ivanovich had cooled somewhat after the episode with the lace and the battle with the pouffe, and he sat there with a scowl on his face. The embarrassment was broken when Sokolov, Ivan Ilyich's footman, came in to report that the plot which Praskovya had chosen in the cemetery was going to cost two hundred roubles. She had stopped weeping, and she looked at Pyotr Ivanovich with a victimized air as she told him in French how hard things were for her. Pyotr Ivanovich made a silent gesture to acknowledge his absolute conviction that it could not be otherwise.

'Do smoke if you would like to,' she said in a tone of voice that was magnanimous yet flat with defeat, and she went on to discuss the cost of the plot with Sokolov. As he lit his cigarette Pyotr Ivanovich heard that she had made detailed inquiries about the cost of various plots of land before settling on the one she wanted. That was not all: once the plot had been ordered she went on to make arrangements for the choir. Then Sokolov left.

'I'm doing everything myself,' she told Pyotr Ivanovich, pushing aside some albums on the table. Noticing that the table was under threat from the cigarette, she swiftly moved an ashtray across and spoke again. 'I think it would be hypocritical to claim that I cannot manage practicalities because of my grief. On the contrary, if anything can . . . I won't say console me, but . . . take my mind off things, it's seeing to what has to be done about him.' She took out her handkerchief again as if on the verge of tears, but suddenly she seemed to get a grip on her feelings, snapped out of it and spoke calmly. 'But there is one thing I would like to discuss with you.'

Pyotr Ivanovich bowed his head. The springs shifted under him, but he did not let them have their way.

'He suffered terribly those last few days.'

'Did he really?' asked Pyotr Ivanovich.

'Oh yes, terribly. The last few minutes, no, hours really, he never stopped screaming. He screamed for three solid days without stopping for breath. It was unbearable. I don't know how I got through it. You could hear him three rooms away. Oh, I've been through it all right!'

'And was he conscious?' asked Pyotr Ivanovich.

'Yes,' she whispered. 'To the very end. He said goodbye a quarter of an hour before he died, and he was still asking us to take Volodya away.'

For all the disagreeable awareness of hypocrisy, his own and hers, the thought of the suffering endured by a man he had known so well, first as a happy young lad, then a schoolboy, then an adult colleague, left Pyotr Ivanovich with a feeling of horror. Once again he could see that forehead, the nose pressing down on the upper lip, and he felt a pang of fear for himself.

'Three days and three nights of horrible suffering, and then death. Just think, it could happen to me any time, now,' he thought and he felt that momentary pang of fear. But immediately he was saved, without knowing how, by the old familiar idea that this had happened to Ivan Ilyich, not him, and it could not and would not happen to him, and that kind of thinking would put him in a gloomy mood, for which there was no need, as Schwartz's face had clearly demonstrated. Pursuing this line of thought Pyotr Ivanovich calmed down and began to show a close interest in the details of Ivan Ilyich's death, as if death was a chance experience that may have applied to Ivan Ilyich but certainly didn't apply to him.

After giving a detailed account of the truly horrendous physical agony that Ivan Ilyich had endured (details that Pyotr Ivanovich learned only in terms of the distressing effect they had had on Praskovya), the widow clearly saw that it was now necessary to get down to business.

'Oh, Pyotr Ivanovich, it's dreadful, absolutely dreadful.' She burst into tears again.

Pyotr Ivanovich gave a sigh, and waited for her to blow her nose. When she had blown her nose, he said, 'Believe me . . .' Then she spoke out again, and told him what must have been the main reason for consulting him: it was all a matter of using the death of her husband to get some money from the Treasury. She made it seem as if she was asking Pyotr Ivanovich's advice about getting a pension, but he could see that here she knew more than he did, she knew the finest details of this subject down to the last penny that could be screwed out of the Treasury in terms of death benefits. What she wanted to know was whether there might be some way of screwing a bit more out of them. Pyotr Ivanovich tried to think of some way of doing this, but having given it some thought and doing the decent thing by cursing the government for being so stingy, he said he thought there was no more to be had. Upon which she gave a sigh, and made no bones about getting rid of her visitor. He got the message, stubbed his cigarette out, stood up, shook hands and went out into the hall.

In the dining-room with the clock that Ivan Ilyich had prided himself on having acquired in an antiques shop Pyotr Ivanovich came across a priest and a number of people that he knew, here for the funeral, and he saw a pretty young lady whom he also knew, Ivan Ilyich's daughter. She was all in black. Her tiny waist looked tinier than ever. She looked gloomy, assertive, almost truculent. She bowed to Pyotr Ivanovich in a way that suggested he was to blame for something. Behind the daughter stood a wealthy young man, also known to Pyotr Ivanovich, who looked no less offended – he was an examining magistrate, her fiancé by all accounts. Pyotr Ivanovich gave a gloomy bow in their direction and was about to walk through into the dead man's room when Ivan Ilyich's schoolboy son, the image of his father, appeared from behind the stairwell. This was the little Ivan Ilyich that Pyotr Ivanovich remembered from law school. His tear-filled eyes were those of a twelve- or thirteen-year-old boy who has lost his innocence. Seeing Pyotr Ivanovich he looked embarrassed, and scowled morosely. Pyotr Ivanovich gave him a nod and walked into the dead man's room. The funeral service was soon under way – candles, moaning, incense, tears, sobbing. Pyotr Ivanovich stood there with a frown on his face, staring at the legs of those in front of him. Not once did he look at the dead man or succumb to any feelings of weakness; he was one of the first to leave. There was no one in the hall. Gerasim, the servant of peasant stock, darted out of the dead man's room, and sorted through all the fur coats with his big strong hands before finding Pyotr Ivanovich's coat and handing it over.

'Gerasim. How are you feeling, my boy?' said Pyotr Ivanovich, who had to say something. 'A bit sad?'

''Tis God's will, sir. 'Twill come to us all,' said Gerasim, displaying an even white row of peasant's teeth, and then, with the air of a man with a lot of work to do, he wrenched the door open, called

13

the driver up and sprang back to the porch steps, wondering what else needed to be done.

Pyotr Ivanovich found it particularly pleasant to inhale the fresh air after the incense, the corpse and carbolic.

'Where to, sir?' asked the coachman.

'It's still quite early. I think I'll drop in on Fyodor Vasilyevich.'

And that's where he went. And there they were, sure enough, finishing the first rubber. He was just in time to make up a fifth.

2

The past history of Ivan Ilyich's life had been straightforward, ordinary and dreadful in the extreme.

Ivan Ilyich had died at forty-five, a member of the Court of Justice. He was the son of an official who had worked his way through various ministries and departments in Petersburg, carving out the kind of career which brings people to a position from which, despite their obvious incapacity for doing anything remotely useful, they cannot be sacked because of their status and long years of service, so they end up being given wholly false and fictitious jobs to do for which they receive salaries that are anything but fictitious, anything from six to ten thousand a year, and this enables them to live on to a ripe old age.

Such a man was Ilya Yefimovich Golovin, Privy Councillor, superfluous member of various superfluous institutions.

He had three sons. Ivan Ilyich was the second son. The eldest had carved out the same career as his father but in a different ministry, and was now near to achieving the kind of seniority that confers sinecure status. The third son was a failure. He had gone through a series of jobs, ruining his prospects in all of them, and he now worked for the railways. His father, his brothers and especially their wives not only hated meeting him but forgot his existence unless compelled to do otherwise. Their sister had married Baron Greff, a Petersburg official cut from the same cloth as his father-in-law. Ivan Ilyich was what they called *le phénix de la famille*. He was neither as cold and starchy as the elder brother nor as profligate as the younger. He was halfway between – an intelligent, lively, personable and decent man. He had attended law school along with his younger brother. The younger brother didn't finish the course; he was expelled in the fifth grade, whereas Ivan Ilyich passed with honours. As a student he was already the kind of person he remained for the rest of his life, a capable man, cheerful and kind, sociable and convinced of the need to follow the path of duty – duty being anything so designated by higher authority. Boy and man he had avoided toadyism, but from his earliest years he was like a moth to the flame in being drawn towards people in authority, he assumed their mannerisms along with their philosophy of life, and he was on good terms with them. All the distractions of childhood and youth had passed him by leaving scarcely a trace; he had succumbed to both sensuality and vanity, and then in the top classes to liberal thinking, but always within limits unerringly set by his own instinctive feelings.

In his student days he had done things that at first he thought of as utterly revolting, things that made him feel disgusted with himself even as he was doing them, but in later life, noticing that the same things were being done by people of high standing without a qualm, although he couldn't quite bring himself to think they were good, he did manage to dismiss them, and he felt no pangs of remorse when he recalled them.

When he graduated from law school, qualifying for the tenth grade of the civil service, and received enough money from his father to buy his basic necessities, Ivan Ilyich ordered a new set of clothes from Scharmer's, hung a medallion on his watch chain inscribed with the words *Respice finem*, said goodbye to the prince and principal, dined at Donon's with his friends, and set off for one of the provinces with his fashionable luggage, linen, clothes, shaving tackle, toiletries and travelling rug, all ordered and purchased from the very best shops, to take up a position arranged for him by his father as special assistant to the governor.

In the provinces it did not take Ivan Ilyich long to arrange a lifestyle that was as easy and agreeable as the one he had enjoyed at law school. He did his work, pursued his career and at the same time discreetly enjoyed himself. He went off now and then on official visits to country districts, cutting a dignified figure with superiors and inferiors alike, and he prided himself on carrying out his duties, especially in matters concerning religious dissidents, with scrupulous fairness and incorruptibility.

In his official duties, despite his youth and an attitude of some frivolity he was exceedingly conservative, bureaucratic and even forbidding, but on the social side he was often amusing and witty, and always pleasantly polite – what the governor and the governor's wife called a *bon enfant*, and with them he was like one of the family.

In the provinces he had an affair with a lady only too keen to liaise with a smart young lawyer. There was also a milliner, and there were drinking sessions with visiting aides-de-camp, as well as after-dinner excursions to a certain street on the outskirts. There was a need to work on the governor and even the governor's wife in order to win them over. But all of this bore the stamp of high respectability to such an extent that no one could have called it by a bad name; all of it was catered for by what the French describe as 'youth having its fling'. All of it was conducted with clean hands, in clean linen, in French phrases, and, what mattered most, at the highest level of society, which meant with approval from those in authority.

Ivan Ilyich spent five years in this kind of service, but the time came for a career change. New legal institutions were opening up; new men were needed.

Ivan Ilyich became one of the new men.

Ivan Ilyich was offered the post of examining magistrate, and he took it, even though it meant moving to a new province, dropping all his old contacts and establishing new ones. Ivan Ilyich was given a send-off by his friends, who presented him with a silver cigarette case, they had a group photograph taken, and off he went to his new job.

As an examining magistrate Ivan Ilyich was just as *comme il faut* and respectable, just as capable of separating official duty from private life and earning respect as he had been when working as a special assistant to the governor. The new work itself struck Ivan Ilyich as far more interesting and rewarding than his earlier job. Before, he had quite liked strutting about in his Scharmer uniform, sauntering past anxious petitioners and envious officials and walking straight into the governor's office, where he would sit down for a cup of tea and a smoke. But not many people had been under his authority – only the rural police chiefs and the religious dissidents that he came across on his assignments – and he loved to treat these dependent people with a courteous, almost comradely spirit, he loved to let them feel that although he had the power to crush them he was being straight with them, treating them like friends. There had not been many of them then, but now that Ivan Ilyich was an examining magistrate he felt that everyone without exception was in his power, even the most important and self-satisfied of people; at a stroke from his pen on headed notepaper any important or self-satisfied person could be brought before him as a defendant or witness to answer questions and be kept on his feet if Ivan Ilyich chose not to let him sit down. Far from abusing this power he did his best to play it down, but his consciousness of that power and the very chance to play it down were what gave his new job its interest and appeal. In the work itself, the process of investigation, Ivan Ilyich soon mastered the technique of distancing himself from all irrelevancies and reducing the most complicated cases to a version that could be set down on paper in objective outline, excluding any personal opinion on his part, while observing all the necessary formalities, which was what mattered most. This was the new way of working, and he was one of the first men to implement the reformed Legal Code of 1864.

Ivan Ilyich's transfer to a new town and the post of examining magistrate meant meeting new people and making new contacts; he also struck a new attitude, and slightly changed his tone. The new attitude involved distancing himself somewhat from the provincial authorities while cultivating the best circles among the judiciary and the wealthy gentry of the town, and the new tone entailed mild dissatisfaction with the government, a degree of liberalism and a civilized man's sense of public duty. At the same time, without compromising the fastidiousness of his dress sense, in his new situation he left his chin unshaven, allowing his beard to grow as and where it wanted.

In his new town, too, Ivan Ilyich set himself up very nicely. The section of society opposed to the governor was friendly and agreeable, his pay had gone up, and one thing that made his life particularly pleasurable was the playing of whist, which he now took to with the enjoyment of a skilled card-player, astute, quick thinking, and almost invariably a winner.

After two years working in the new town Ivan Ilyich met his future wife. Praskovya Fyodorovna Mikhel was the most attractive, intelligent and colourful young lady in the social circle frequented by Ivan Ilyich. To the list of other distractions and relaxations from his work as an examining magistrate Ivan Ilyich added a mild flirtation with Praskovya.

When he had been an assistant on special commissions Ivan Ilyich had been quite a dancer, but now he was an examining magistrate he took to the floor much less frequently. When he danced it was only as if to say, 'Look, I may be part of the reformed system, and I've got as far as Grade 5, but if you want to see me on the floor I can show you that even in dancing I can be the best.' So, just occasionally, he would take to the floor with Praskovya at the end of an evening, and it was actually while dancing like this that he won her heart. She fell in love with him. Ivan Ilyich had no clear and definite plans for marriage, but once the girl fell in love with him he began to wonder. 'When all's said and done, why shouldn't I get married?' he asked himself.

This young woman, Praskovya Fyodorovna, belonged to a good family, and she was quite attractive. She also came with a little money. Ivan Ilyich might have held out for a more brilliant partner, but she was herself a decent catch. Ivan was earning good money, and he could count on something similar from her. It would be a good match – she was a nice girl, quite pretty and a thoroughly decent young woman. To claim that Ivan Ilyich got married because he was in love with his bride, and saw in her someone who shared his outlook on life, would have been no more justifiable than to say that he married because the match met with the approval of the society that he moved in. Ivan Ilyich married for both reasons. He was pleasing himself by acquiring such a wife, but at the same time he was appealing to his superiors and their sense of propriety.

So, Ivan Ilyich got married.

The process of getting married, and the early days of married life, with conjugal caresses, new furniture, new crockery, new linen, everything up to his wife's pregnancy, went very smoothly, to the extent that Ivan Ilyich was beginning to think that marriage would not disrupt his easy, agreeable and enjoyable lifestyle, which was decency itself, approved of by society and something that Ivan Ilyich considered to be part of life itself – and it might even improve it. But it was at this stage, during the first months of his wife's pregnancy, that something happened, something new, unexpected, unpleasant, difficult and disgusting, something that could not have been anticipated and could not in any way be got rid of.

For no reason that Ivan Ilyich could fathom,

other than what he called *gaîté de coeur*, his wife did begin to disrupt the pleasant and decent running of his life. She became jealous of him for no apparent cause, demanded his closest attention, laid into him and started arguments that were unpleasantly vulgar.

At first Ivan Ilyich hoped to escape the unpleasantness of his new situation by relapsing into the same carefree but respectable way of life that had stood him in good stead before – he tried to ignore his wife's moodiness and carry on in the easy, agreeable way that he had formerly enjoyed, inviting friends round for a game of cards and trying to get out and drive round to the club or visit people close to him. But there came a time when his wife started shouting at him so furiously, using such foul language, determined to keep on yelling at him when he failed to do what she wanted, obviously with every intention of keeping it up until he came to heel, stayed in and went through the same anguish that she felt, that Ivan Ilyich was horrified. He realized that married life – at least with his wife – didn't always mean enjoyment and decency, but, on the contrary it often disrupted them, and it was therefore necessary to guard against such disruptions. And Ivan Ilyich began to seek ways of doing this. His work was the one thing that impressed Praskovya, and it was through work and the commitments associated with it that he took on his wife and asserted his own independence.

When the baby was born, with the various difficulties with feeding, the real and imaginary illnesses of mother and child, which demanded his sympathetic involvement even though he understood nothing about them, the need for Ivan Ilyich to safeguard his independence became even more urgent.

As his wife grew more and more irritable and demanding, Ivan Ilyich gradually shifted his life's centre of gravity on to his work. He loved his work more and more, and became more ambitious than he had been.

It didn't take him long – no more than a year after his wedding – to realize that although married life did provide some conveniences, it was actually rather a complex and difficult business, and the path of duty, which meant leading a decent life approved of by society, called for a clearly defined attitude, as at work.

And Ivan Ilyich managed to establish such an attitude towards his married life. He required of it whatever domestic conveniences it could provide in terms of meals on the table, a good household and a bed, and, most important, the outward show of respectability that society required. Beyond this, he sought some enjoyment and pleasure, and if he found this he was very thankful, but if he was met with rejection and crabbiness he immediately took himself off into his own separate, carefully guarded world, the world of work which gave him pleasure.

Ivan Ilyich was considered a good colleague, and within three years he was promoted to assistant chief prosecutor. His new responsibilities, the importance that they entailed, the opportunity of bringing people before the court and sending them to prison, the publicity given to his speeches, and the success enjoyed by Ivan Ilyich in these matters – all of this made his work seem even more enjoyable.

Other children were born. His wife was becoming more and more bad tempered and crabby, but the new attitude established by Ivan Ilyich towards his home life made him all but impervious to her crabbiness.

After serving for seven years in the same town Ivan Ilyich was transferred to another province, as public prosecutor. They moved, they were short of money, and his wife didn't like the town they had moved to. His salary had gone up, but so had their living expenses. On top of that, two of their children died, and family life became even more unpleasant for Ivan Ilyich.

Praskovya blamed her husband for all the setbacks they were suffering in their new place of residence. Most of the topics of conversation between husband and wife, especially about bringing up the children, led to questions that reminded them of past arguments, and new arguments were liable to flare up at any moment. They were left with a few short periods of amorousness that came over them as husband and wife, but these did not last long. These were nothing more than little islands where they could anchor for a while, only to plunge back into a sea of hidden hostility as they grew further and further apart. This growing apart might have upset Ivan Ilyich if he had thought there was anything wrong with it, but now not only did he consider this state of affairs to be quite normal, he saw it as the whole point of his role in the family. His role was to distance himself increasingly from all the unpleasantness and give it an air of harmless respectability; this he achieved by spending less and less time with the family, and when he was forced to be with them he sought to safeguard his own position by ensuring the presence of others. But the main thing was that Ivan Ilyich did have his work. It was in the world of his work that the whole interest of his life came into focus. And this interest absorbed him totally. The knowledge of the power that he wielded, the possibility of ruining anyone that he fancied ruining, the gravitas (even if it was all outward show) which could be sensed as he walked into court or dealt with his subordinates, the success that he was enjoying with his superiors and subordinates alike, and, above all, his masterly handling of the cases – all of this gave him pleasure, and, along with chit-chat with colleagues, dinners and whist, filled his life to the full. And so, life in general proceeded for Ivan Ilyich just as he thought it should proceed – pleasantly and respectably.

He lived like this for about seven years. Their daughter, the eldest child, was now sixteen, another child had died and their one remaining son was the subject of strong disagreement. Ivan Ilyich wanted to send him to law school, but Praskovya had defied him by putting him down for the high school. The daughter was being educated at home, and was developing nicely; the boy too was doing quite well at his studies.

3

This was the course that Ivan Ilyich's life had taken
during the seventeen years that followed his
wedding. He was now a senior public prosecutor
who had turned down several transfers in the hope
of securing an even more desirable position, but
then suddenly an unpleasant circumstance arose
which looked like completely disrupting the
peaceful progress of his life. Ivan Ilyich was
expecting an appointment as presiding judge in a
university town, but Hoppe pipped him at the post
and got the job. Ivan Ilyich was livid, and he made
some insinuations, taking issue with Hoppe
himself and his immediate superiors. He was met
with a chill rebuff, and was overlooked again when
the next appointment came up.

This was in 1880. That year was the hardest he
ever lived through. It was a year in which it trans-
pired, for one thing, that they couldn't make ends
meet financially, and, for another, that he was a
forgotten man, and whereas he saw himself as the
victim of an outrageously cruel injustice everyone
else thought it was just the way things went. Even
his father saw it as no duty of his to help out. He
felt deserted by everyone; they all thought that his
situation, with a salary of 3500 roubles, was perfectly

normal, even fortunate. He was the only person who knew that, with all the injustices that had been visited upon him, with nothing but nagging from his wife, and the debts that were now mounting up because he was living beyond his means – he was the only one who knew that his position was anything but normal.

That summer, in order to cut costs, he took leave of absence and went with his wife for a country holiday at her brother's place. In the country, with no work to occupy him, Ivan Ilyich had his first experience of not just boredom but unbearable anguish. He decided he couldn't go on like this – definite steps must be taken.

During a sleepless night, the whole of which he spent pacing the terrace, he decided he would go to Petersburg and make representations; he would get his own back on *those men* who had underestimated him, by changing ministries. Next morning he defied all the remonstrations from his wife and brother-in-law and left for Petersburg.

He went with one aim in mind: to get himself a position that would bring in five thousand a year. By now he had no allegiance to any particular ministry, faction or function. All he needed was a job, a job that would bring in five thousand a year, in administration, in one of the banks, with the railways, in one of the charitable institutions set up by the Dowager Empress Maria, even in the customs service; all that mattered was five thousand a year and an immediate transfer from the ministry where he was so undervalued.

And his trip was crowned with unexpected, unbelievable success. At Kursk, an acquaintance of his, F. S. Ilyin, got into his first-class carriage, sat down and told him that the governor of the province had just received a telegram informing him of a reshuffle in the ministry – Pyotr Ivanovich was being replaced by Ivan Semyonovich.

The proposed reshuffle, whatever its impact on Russia at large, meant something special to Ivan Ilyich: the emergence of Pyotr Petrovich, and also apparently his friend, Zakhar Ivanovich, was very good news for him. Zakhar Ivanovich was a colleague and friend.

The new development had been confirmed in Moscow; now, arriving in Petersburg, Ivan Ilyich looked up Zakhar, who promised him a definite position in his former department, the Ministry of Justice.

Within a week he was able to send the following telegram to his wife: *Zakhar replaces Miller. Appointment mine with first report.*

Because of this change of staff Ivan Ilyich had suddenly achieved a position in his former ministry which put him two grades higher than his colleagues with five thousand a year plus 3500 roubles removal expenses. All the acrimony that he had felt towards his enemies and the ministry in general was forgotten, and Ivan Ilyich was a happy man.

He returned to the country in high spirits, more

contented than he had been for a long time. Praskovya's spirits had also picked up, and a truce was declared between the two of them. Ivan Ilyich described how honoured he had been in Petersburg, how his former enemies had been put to shame and were now licking his boots, how people envied him his new position, and, most of all, how popular he had been in Petersburg.

Praskovya listened to all of this, pretending to believe it and not querying anything, but her real interest was only in sketching out the new way of life that they would lead in the city to which they were moving. And Ivan Ilyich was delighted to see that her plans were his plans, they were together as one, and that his life, having hit a bad patch, was now getting back to its old way, its true path of happy enjoyment and respectability.

Ivan Ilyich had not come back for long. He had to take up his duties on 10 September, and before that he had to settle into new surroundings, have all his things brought in from the provinces, buy in and order up many more items – in other words to set up home just as he had worked things out in his own mind, which was almost exactly as Praskovya had worked things out in her own heart.

And now that everything had been set up so successfully, and he and his wife were agreed in their aims, having lived together so little of late, they came together more closely than at any time since they were first married. Ivan Ilyich had intended to move his family in straightaway, but at the insistence of his sister-in-law and brother-in-law, who were suddenly all over Ivan Ilyich and his family, it was arranged for him to go on alone.

Ivan Ilyich set out on his journey. The happy feelings brought on by his success and a rapprochement with his wife, each intensifying the other, never left him. He found a delightful place, a dream apartment for him and his wife. The spacious, high-ceilinged reception rooms with their old-fashioned décor, the gracefully appointed and comfortable study, the rooms for his wife and daughter, the classroom for his son – all of it seemed to have been designed with them in mind. Ivan Ilyich took it upon himself to organize the fittings and furnishings; he chose the wallpaper, purchased furniture, predominantly of the old-fashioned style which he considered to be *comme il faut*, the upholstery . . . and the whole thing grew and grew, approaching the ideal that he had set himself. Even halfway through the refurbishment, the whole thing exceeded his expectations. He could see how elegant it would all be, quite *comme il faut* and devoid of vulgarity, when it was completed. As he went to sleep he would imagine what the large reception room was going to look like. When he glanced into the half-finished drawing-room he could envisage the fireplace, the screen, the whatnot and the little chairs dotted about the room, the plates and dishes on the walls and the bronze pieces, everything in its proper place. He enjoyed the thought of surprising Pasha and Lizanka, who were not without taste themselves. This was beyond their expectations. He had been particularly successful in tracking down antiques and buying them at bargain prices; they now gave the whole place an air of distinction. He deliberately understated everything in his letters home so that they would be surprised. He was so taken up with all of this that the work he loved so dearly interested him less than he had thought it would. In court he found his mind wandering; he would be miles away, wondering whether to have plain or moulded cornices with his curtains. He became so involved that he often did the work himself, rearranging the furniture and rehanging the curtains. On one occasion, climbing a stepladder to show a dull-witted upholsterer how to hang the draperies, he slipped and fell, though he was strong and agile enough to hold on, and all he did was bump his side on a window-frame knob. The bruising hurt for a while but it soon passed off. And all this time Ivan Ilyich felt particularly well and in the best of spirits. 'I seem to have shed fifteen years,' he wrote home. He had hoped to get it all finished by the end of September but things dragged on until mid-October. Still, it was magnificent, and he wasn't the only one to say so – everybody did.

But these were essentially the accoutrements that appeal to all people who are not actually rich but who want to look rich, though all they manage to do is look like each other: damasks, ebony, plants, rugs and bronzes, anything dark and gleaming – everything that all people of a certain class affect so as to be like all other people of a certain class. And his arrangements looked so much like everyone else's that they were unremarkable, though he saw them as something truly distinctive. When he met his family at the railway station, brought them home and ushered them into his well-lit furnished apartment and a footman wearing a white tie opened the door into the entrance hall decorated with flowers, and then they went into the drawing-room and the study, ooh-ing and ah-ing with delight, he was a very happy man, showing them around everywhere, revelling in their praise and beaming with delight. That evening as they took tea, when Praskovya asked him casually about his fall he gave a laugh and demonstrated how he had gone flying and given the upholsterer a scare.

'It's a good job I'm athletic. Any other man would have killed himself, but all I did was bruise myself a bit here. It's hurts when you touch it, but it's getting better. It is only a bruise.'

And so they began life in their new abode, where, as always happens with people who have recently settled in, they found themselves just one room short, and their new income wouldn't quite run to it, though it was only a matter of five hundred roubles or so. Still, they were very nicely off, especially during the early days when not everything was finished and work was still to be done – things had to be bought, ordered, rearranged, adjusted. There were one or two disagreements between husband and wife, but both of them were so satisfied and so busy that everything resolved itself without serious arguments. When there was nothing more to be finished off they developed a feeling of dullness and a sense of something missing, but by this time they had got to know new people and formed new habits. Their lives had filled out.

Ivan Ilyich would return for lunch after a morning in court and in those early days he tended to be in a good mood; any slight distress that he suffered came from the apartment itself. (The slightest stain on a tablecloth or upholstery, or a loose cord on the draperies annoyed him; he had put so much effort into the furnishings that the slightest disturbance upset him.) But all things considered Ivan Ilyich's life went along, as he saw it, just as life ought to go – easily, pleasantly, decently. He rose at nine, drank some coffee, read the newspaper, then put on his uniform and went to court. There, the collar that he worked in had been worn into shape and he soon found that it fitted him well – the petitioners, the inquiries received, the office, the public sessions and the administrative meetings. In all of this the trick was to eliminate the element of crude everyday life that always disrupts the smooth flow of official business; no relationships should be entered into beyond the official ones, the reason behind any relationship had to be strictly official and the relationship itself had to be strictly official. Say, for example, a person arrives wanting to know something. This is not the responsibility of Ivan Ilyich; he can have no relationship with such a person. But if this person were to approach him in his capacity as a member of the judiciary and in a relationship that can be set down on letterhead paper, within the terms of that relationship Ivan Ilyich will do anything he can, and do it decisively, while maintaining a semblance of friendly human relations – nothing more than common courtesy. At the point where an official relationship breaks off everything else breaks off too. The skill of compartmentalizing the official side of things and keeping that apart from his own real life was one that Ivan Ilyich possessed in the highest degree; long practice and natural talent had enabled him to refine it to such a degree that now he could act like a virtuoso performer, occasionally allowing himself to mix human and official relationships by way of a joke. He allowed himself this liberty because he felt strong enough whenever necessary to reinstate the distinction between the official and the human by discarding the latter. This was more than just an easy, pleasant and decent thing for Ivan Ilyich to do – he was acting like an expert performer. During his breaks he would have a smoke, drink tea and chat, exchange a word or two about politics, current affairs and cards, and a whole lot more about who was in and who was out. And he would go home tired, but feeling like a virtuoso performer, a first violin in the orchestra, who has given of his best. At home his daughter and his wife would either have been out visiting or would have entertained someone at home, while his son, back from school, would have had a session with his private tutors and gone on to cram whatever it is they teach in schools. Everything was fine. After dinner, if there were no guests, Ivan Ilyich sometimes read a book that people were talking about, and later in the evening sat down to do some work, reading through papers, studying the law, comparing depositions and sorting them by statute. This neither bored nor amused him. He found it boring when he might have been playing whist, but if whist was off it was better than just sitting there on his own or with his wife. What gave Ivan Ilyich real pleasure, though, was giving little dinner parties to which he would invite ladies and gentlemen of good social standing and passing the time with them precisely as such people invariably do pass the time, in the way that his drawing-room was exactly like all the others.

One day they held an evening party with dancing. Ivan Ilyich enjoyed it, and everything went swimmingly, except for a big row between him and his wife over the cakes and sweets. Praskovya had had her own ideas, but Ivan Ilyich had insisted on bringing in an expensive caterer who had provided too many cakes; the leftovers had caused the row when the caterer's bill came to forty-five roubles. The row was a big one, very nasty, and it ended with Praskovya calling him a stupid fool while he clutched his head and muttered something about divorce. But he still enjoyed the party. The best people were there and Ivan Ilyich danced with Princess Trufonova, whose sister had famously founded the charity known as 'Take Away my Sorrow'. Pleasure derived from work was self-indulgence, pleasure derived from socializing tickled his vanity, but real pleasure came to Ivan Ilyich only from playing cards. He was prepared to admit that, at the end of the day, with any amount of unpleasantness behind him, the one pleasure that outshone all others like a beacon was to sit down and play whist with quiet-mannered partners, good players, always in a foursome (sitting out was such a bore when there were five, and you had to pretend not to mind), and playing seriously and playing well (when you got a decent hand) before going on to supper with a glass of wine. And after a game of cards, especially if he had won a small amount (big winnings were not nice), Ivan Ilyich would go to bed in the very best of spirits.

This was how they lived. They moved in the best of circles, receiving people of quality, and the younger set.

In their attitude towards the circle of their acquaintances husband, wife and daughter were of one mind. Without collusion each of them in the same way shrugged off and discarded all the shabby friends and relatives who flocked around fawning on them in the drawing-room with the Japanese plates on the walls. It wasn't long before the shabby friends stopped flocking around and left the Golovin family to the best people in society and no one else. Young men were attracted to their little Liza and one examining magistrate by the name of Petrishchev, the son of Dmitriy Ivanovich Petrishchev and his sole heir, became so attentive towards her that Ivan Ilyich mentioned this once or twice to Praskovya and wondered whether they ought perhaps to take them out for a ride in a troika or set up some private theatricals. This was how they lived. This was how things went, nothing changed and everything was fine.

4

They were all in good health. The fact that Ivan Ilyich sometimes complained of a strange taste in his mouth and a funny feeling in his left side didn't count as ill health.

But as it happened this funny feeling began to get worse and turned into, if not pain exactly, a constant dragging sensation in his side, which put him in a bad mood. And this bad mood, which got worse and worse, began to spoil the pleasant, easy-going and respectable way of life that the Golovins had just set up for themselves. There were more and more quarrels between husband and wife, the pleasant, easy-going way of things lapsed, and they were hard put to keep up an appearance of decency. Once again scenes became more and more frequent. They were left once again with nothing more than those little islands, all too few of them, on which husband and wife could come together without an explosion.

And now Praskovya began to say, not without justification, that her husband was a hard man. With her usual capacity for exaggeration she claimed that he had always been horrible like that and only her good nature had enabled her to put up with it for twenty years. It was true that all the arguments now began on his side. His jibes always started just as they sat down to dinner, often over the soup. There was always something – if it wasn't chipped crockery or something wrong with the food he would go on about his son putting his elbow on the table or his daughter's hair. And it was always Praskovya's fault. To begin with Praskovya would take issue with him and say something nasty, but on a couple of occasions he flew into such a rage at the beginning of dinner that she realized this was a pathological condition brought on by consuming food so she bit it all back, stopped objecting and got on with her dinner as fast as she could. Praskovya took great pride in biting things back. Convinced that her husband was a horrible man who had made her life a misery, she was now sorry for herself. And the sorrier she became, the more she hated her husband. She began to wish he was dead, and then not to, because without him there would be no income. All of which made her even more exasperated with him. She felt thoroughly miserable at the thought that not even his death could rescue her. She was exasperated, though she hid it, but her hidden exasperation served only to strengthen his exasperation.

After one scene during which Ivan Ilyich had been particularly unfair and after which, by way of explanation, he had admitted being exasperating but claimed he was ill, she told him that if he was ill he needed treatment and insisted that he must go and see a famous doctor.

He did. The whole thing turned out just as he had expected, and as it always does. He was made to wait, the doctor was full of his own importance – an attitude he was familiar with because it was one that he himself assumed in court – then came all the tapping and listening, the questions with predetermined and obviously superfluous answers, the knowing look that seemed to say, 'Just place yourself in our hands and we'll sort it out, we know what we're doing, there's no doubt about it, we can sort things out the same way as we would for anyone you care to name.' It was just like being in court. The way he looked at the accused in court was exactly the way he was being looked at now by the famous doctor.

The doctor was holding forth. Such and such demonstrates that in your inside there is such and such, but if this is not confirmed by our tests on this and that then you will need to go on to such and such. And if you go on to such and such, then . . . and so on. As far as Ivan Ilyich was concerned there was only one question that mattered: 'Is this condition life-threatening or not?' But the doctor treated this question as irrelevant, and ignored it. From the doctor's point of view it was a pointless question not worthy of discussion; the only thing was a balancing of probabilities – floating kidney, chronic colitis, problem with the blind gut. The question of Ivan Ilyich living or dying didn't arise; there was just this conflict between the floating kidney and the blind gut. And before his very eyes the doctor resolved the conflict at a brilliant stroke in favour of the floating kidney, with the sole proviso that new evidence might emerge from the urine test, and if that happened the case would have to be reviewed. All of it from start to finish was precisely what Ivan Ilyich himself had done to the accused a thousand times and with no less brilliance. Brilliant indeed was the doctor's summing up of the situation as he looked in triumph bordering on delight over his glasses at his own prisoner in the dock. From the summary Ivan Ilyich drew only one conclusion: he was in a bad way, and the doctor didn't care, nobody cared probably, but he was in a bad way. And this conclusion left Ivan Ilyich with a sickly feeling, filling him with self-pity and great animosity towards the doctor who showed so much indifference to such an important question.

But he said nothing about it. He got up, laid his money on the table, and said with a sigh, 'I'm sure that when we're ill we ask a lot of pointless questions. But, er, is it life-threatening or not . . . ?'

The doctor glared at him through one eye over his glasses as if to say, 'Prisoner in the dock, if you will not confine yourself to answering the questions put to you I shall have to arrange for you to be removed from the courtroom.'

'I have already told you what I consider necessary and appropriate. Anything further will be determined by the tests.' The doctor bowed.

Ivan Ilyich walked out slowly, climbed gloomily

into his sledge and drove home. All the way back he kept going over in his mind everything the doctor had said, trying to translate his confusingly complex technicalities into everyday speech and find in them an answer to one question: am I in a bad way, a really bad way, or is it nothing to worry about just now? And it seemed to him that the message from all that the doctor had said was yes, you're in a very bad way. Ivan Ilyich thought the streets looked dismal. The drivers looked dismal, the houses looked dismal, and so did the pedestrians and the shops. And in the light of the doctor's confusing pronouncements the pain, that dull nagging pain that never went away, was taking on a new and more serious significance. It was with a new feeling of dejection that Ivan Ilyich focused on it.

He reached home and started to tell his wife. His wife listened closely, but halfway through his account their daughter came in wearing a little hat – she and her mother were on their way out. She made an effort to sit down and listen to his boring story, but she couldn't contain herself for long and her mother gave up listening.

'Well, I'm very pleased,' said his wife. 'And now, you listen to me. Make sure you take your medicine properly. Give me the prescription and I'll send Gerasim to the chemist's.' And she went off to get dressed.

He had hardly paused for breath while she was in the room, and when she went out he gave a deep sigh.

'Oh well,' he said. 'Maybe that's right. Nothing to worry about just now . . .'

He started taking his medicine and following the doctor's instructions, though these were changed once the urine test results were in. But at this point it turned out that there was some confusion over the test itself and what was supposed to follow it. Without getting at the doctor, it was becoming clear that what was going on was not what the doctor had said. He must have overlooked something, or he had been telling lies, or he was hiding something.

Nevertheless, Ivan Ilyich started to follow his instructions, and from the process of doing so he derived some comfort for a while. Since his visit to the doctor Ivan Ilyich had made it his main preoccupation to follow all instructions to the letter in matters of hygiene, the taking of medicine, focusing on his pain and monitoring all his bodily functions. His main interests were in human sickness and human health. When he overheard anyone talking about people who had fallen ill, died or recovered, especially if the illness sounded like his own, he tried to hide his agitation but he listened closely, asked lots of questions and applied what he heard to his own illness.

The pain was not getting any less, but Ivan Ilyich made every effort to make himself believe he was feeling better. And he was able to delude himself as long as nothing upset him. But the moment he fell out with his wife, or something went wrong at work or he got a bad hand at whist, he felt the full force

of his illness. Before this he had been able to with-
stand setbacks like these, expecting to put things
right before long, to win through, succeed again,
come out with a grand slam. But now the slightest
setback cut the ground from under him and left him
in despair. He would say to himself, 'Look at that.
I was just starting to get better, and the medicine
was just beginning to work, and now this damn
thing comes up, this rotten luck . . .' And he raged
against his misfortune or against those people who
were causing his problems and killing him off; he
sensed that it was his own rage that was killing him
and he couldn't control it. It ought to have been
obvious to him that raging against his situation and
the people around him was only feeding his illness
and because of that he ought to ignore any
unpleasant developments, but he thought the exact
opposite: he told himself he needed peace of mind
so he had to get on to anything that disrupted his
peace of mind, and the slightest disruption left him
exasperated. His situation was made worse by the
fact that he had taken to reading medical books and
consulting doctors. The decline was so gradual that
he was able to delude himself by comparing one
day with another and seeing little difference. But the
moment he consulted a doctor he thought he was
going downhill, and fast. Yet despite this he kept on
consulting the doctors.

That month he went to see another celebrity. This
celebrity told him more or less the same as the first
one, but put things differently. And the consultation

with this celebrity served only to reinforce Ivan Ilyich's doubts and fears. A friend of a friend – a very good doctor – diagnosed something entirely different, and even though he swore he would get better his questions and assumptions confused Ivan Ilyich even more and deepened his suspicions. A homeopath produced yet another diagnosis and gave him some medicine, which Ivan Ilyich took for a week or so without telling anyone. But by the end of the week, feeling no better and losing faith in every treatment that had been prescribed so far including that one, he felt more despondent than ever. One day a lady of his acquaintance talked to him about the curative powers of icons. Ivan Ilyich caught himself listening closely to what she was saying, and beginning to accept it as fact. This scared him. 'Am I really going weak in the head?' he wondered. 'Nonsense. It's all rubbish! I'm not falling for stupid ideas like that. I'd rather pick one doctor and stick to what he says. That's what I'm going to do. That's it. I'm going to stop thinking about it, and follow the treatment to the letter until the summer. Then we'll see. No more shilly-shallying.' This was easy to say but impossible to do. The pain in his side went on wearing him down and seemed to be getting worse, nagging incessantly, while the taste in his mouth got more and more peculiar and he began to think that his breath smelt awful, and his appetite and strength fell away. The time for fooling himself was over: something new and dreadful was going on inside Ivan Ilyich, something significant, more significant than anything in his whole life. And he was the only one who knew it; the people around him didn't know, or didn't want to know – they thought that everything in the world was going on as before. This was what tormented Ivan Ilyich more than anything. He could see that his family, especially his wife and daughter, whose visiting season was in full swing, had no inkling; it annoyed them that he was not much fun and asked so much of them – as if he was to blame. Despite their best efforts to hide it, he could see that he was in their way. His wife had developed an attitude to his illness and she was sticking to it whatever he might say or do. Her attitude went like this: 'You know what it's like,' she would say to her friends, 'Ivan Ilyich can't be like other people. He won't stick to his treatment. One moment he takes his drops and eats what he's supposed to, and goes to bed when he should – the next day, if I'm not watching him, he doesn't take his medicine, he eats sturgeon, which he's not allowed, and he stays up playing whist until one in the morning.'

'Oh come on,' says Ivan Ilyich. 'I did that once, with Pyotr Ivanovich.'

'What about yesterday, with Shebek?'

'It made no difference. I couldn't sleep with all that pain . . .'

'Well, it doesn't matter why. Only you'll never get better like that, and it's getting us down.'

Praskovya's attitude towards Ivan Ilyich's illness, of which she made no secret to other people or to him, was that it was all his fault; he was making his wife's life a misery yet again. Ivan Ilyich felt she was doing this unconsciously, but that didn't make things any easier for him.

In court Ivan Ilyich noticed, or thought he noticed, the same strange attitude towards him. There were times when he thought people were watching him closely like a man who was about to give up his job; at other times his associates would make friendly little jokes about the way he worried over his health, as if this ghastly, fearful, unheard-of thing that had got going inside him and was now incessantly gnawing at him and inexorably taking him away was a good subject and a laughing matter. The one who infuriated him most was Schwartz, with his playfulness, *joie de vivre* and all-round respectability which recalled the Ivan Ilyich of ten years before.

His friends have come round for a game of cards. They take their places and deal, softening the new cards. He sorts his diamonds – seven of them. His partner bids no trumps and supports him with two diamonds. Couldn't be better. This should be a wonderful, joyous moment – a grand slam is on. But suddenly he feels that gnawing pain, that taste in his mouth, and he is struck by the barbarity of rejoicing in a grand slam.

He glances across at his partner, Mikhail Mikhaylovich, who is tapping the table with an eager hand, politely and graciously holding back from grabbing the tricks and pushing them towards Ivan Ilyich so that he can enjoy the pleasure of raking them in without having to make any effort or reaching very far. 'Does he think I'm too weak to reach out?' thinks Ivan Ilyich, forgetting what are trumps and overtrumping his partner with his own, which leaves them three tricks short of a grand slam. And worst of all, he can see how upset Mikhail Mikhaylovich is, and he doesn't care. And it is awful to think why he doesn't care.

They can all see that he is distraught, and they say to him, 'We can stop if you're feeling tired. Why don't you have a rest?' Rest? No, he's *not tired*. They finish the rubber. They are all gloomy and silent. Ivan Ilyich senses that he has caused the gloom, and he cannot dispel it. They have supper and go home, and Ivan Ilyich is left there alone with the knowledge that his life has been poisoned and is poisoning other people's lives, and the poison is not wearing off, it is working its way deeper and deeper into his very being.

And he has to take this knowledge to bed with him, along with the physical pain and the terror, often to spend a near-sleepless night because of the pain. And next morning he has to get up again, put on his clothes, go to court, talk, write, or, if he doesn't go out, stay in with every one of those twenty-four hours that make up a day and a night, each one of them an agony. And he has to live like this on the edge of destruction, alone, with nobody at all to understand and pity him.

5

One month passed like this, then another. His brother-in-law came to town and stayed with them for the New Year celebrations. Ivan Ilyich was in court when he arrived. Praskovya was out shopping. On his return Ivan Ilyich walked into his study and found his son-in-law already there, a strong, fit young man, busy unpacking his own suitcase. He looked up when he heard Ivan Ilyich approaching and stared at him in silence for a moment. That stare told Ivan Ilyich everything. His brother-in-law opened his mouth to exclaim, but managed to restrain himself. That movement confirmed everything.

'I've changed, haven't I?'

'Well . . . you have rather.'

And after this, however hard Ivan Ilyich tried to raise the subject of his appearance, his brother-in-law wouldn't say a word. Praskovya arrived home and her brother went to see her. Ivan Ilyich locked the door and went to have a good look at himself in the mirror, full-face, then in profile. He picked up a photograph of himself with his wife and compared his likeness with what he now saw in the mirror. The difference was enormous. Then he pulled his sleeves up, looked at his arms, pulled his sleeves back down and sat down on an ottoman, looking blacker than night.

'No, no. I mustn't,' he told himself. He jumped up and went to his desk, where he opened a file and began to read, but he couldn't go on. He opened the door and went out into the hallway. The door into the drawing-room was shut. He tiptoed over to it and started to listen.

'No, you're exaggerating,' Praskovya was saying.

'What do you mean, exaggerating? You can't see it. He's a dead man. Look at his eyes – there's no light in them. What is it he's got exactly?'

'Nobody knows. Nikolayev [yet another doctor] said something, but I don't know what it was. Leshchetitsky [the celebrity] said the exact opposite . . .'

Ivan Ilyich walked away back into his room, lay down and started to think things over. 'Kidney, a floating kidney . . .' He could remember everything the doctors had told him about it becoming detached and starting to wander. With an effort of his imagination he tried to catch the kidney, stop it moving and fix it strongly. It seemed to take so little effort. 'No, I'm going back Pyotr Ivanovich [the friend who was the doctor's friend].' He rang the bell, ordered the carriage and prepared to go out.

'*Jean*, where are you going?' asked his wife, looking very gloomy but uncharacteristically kind.

The uncharacteristic kindness infuriated him. He gave her a dark look.

'I've got to go and see Pyotr Ivanovich.'

He went to see the friend with the friend who was the doctor, and on with him to the doctor himself, who was in. They had a long talk.

Going through the details of anatomy and physiology in terms of what the doctor considered to be happening in his insides made everything quite clear to him.

There was a little bit of something, a tiny little thing, in his blind gut. It could all be put right. By raising the energy level in one organ and lowering the activity of another, absorption could be achieved, and everything would be all right. He was a little late for dinner. He talked cheerfully after dinner, but for some time he couldn't bring himself to go to his room and work. Eventually he did go off to his study and he got straight down to it. He worked at the files for a while, but he couldn't shrug off the awareness that he had some important unfinished personal business that would have to be attended to in the end. When he had finished the files he remembered that this personal business meant thinking about his gut. But instead of giving in to this he went to take tea in the drawing-room. They had guests – there was conversation, pianoplaying and singing – and among them was the examining magistrate who was such a good match for his daughter. As Praskovya remarked, he enjoyed the evening more than usual, but never for a minute did he forget that he had some important unfinished thinking to do, about his gut. At eleven o'clock he said goodnight and went to his room. He had been sleeping alone since his illness began, in a tiny little room next to his study. He went in, undressed and took up a Zola novel, but instead of reading it he lapsed into thought. And in his imagination the longed-for healing of his blind gut took place; absorption was followed by evacuation and its proper function was restored. 'Yes, that's how it goes,' he said to himself, 'All you have to do is give nature a helping hand.' He remembered his medicine, eased himself up and took it, then lay on his back focusing on the good that the medicine was doing and the way it was getting rid of the pain. 'Keep taking it regularly and avoid anything harmful. I feel a bit better already, a lot better.' He felt his side – no pain to the touch. 'No, there's no feeling there. It really is getting a lot better.' He put out the candle and lay on his side . . .

Absorption; the blind gut was curing itself. Then suddenly he could feel the same old dull gnawing pain, quiet, serious, unrelenting. The same nasty taste in his mouth. His heart sank and his head swam. 'O God! O God!' he muttered, 'It's here again, and it's not going away.' And suddenly he saw things from a completely different angle. 'The blind gut! The kidney!' he said to himself. 'It's got nothing to do with the blind gut or the kidney. It's a matter of living or . . . dying. Yes, I have been alive, and now my life is steadily going away, and I can't stop it. No. There's no point in fooling myself. Can't they all see – everybody but me –

that I'm dying? It's only a matter of weeks, or days – maybe any minute now. There has been daylight; now there is darkness. I have been *here*; now I'm going *there*. Where?' A cold shiver ran over him; he stopped breathing. He could hear nothing but the beating of his heart.

'When I'm dead, what happens then? Nothing happens. So where shall I be when I'm no longer here? Is this really death? No, I won't have it!' He jumped up, tried to light the candle, fumbling with trembling hands, dropped the candle and the stick on the floor and flopped back down on to his pillow. 'Why bother? It doesn't make any difference,' he said to himself, staring into the darkness with his eyes wide open. 'Death. Yes, it's death. And not one of them knows, or wants to know. They have no pity for me. Too busy playing.' (Through the door he could hear the distant sounds of a singing voice and the accompaniment.) 'They don't care, but they're going to die too. Fools! Me first, then them, but they've got it coming to them. And they're enjoying themselves! Animals!' He was choking with spite. And he felt a wave of agonizing, unbearable misery. It surely wasn't possible that everybody everywhere should be condemned to this awful horror. He sat up.

'Something's not right. I've got to calm down and think it through from the beginning.' And he began to think. 'Yes, the beginning of the illness. I banged my side, but I felt just the same that day and the next. A bit of discomfort, then a bit more,

57

then doctors, depression, worry, more doctors, and all the time I was getting nearer and nearer to the edge. Less and less strength. Nearer and nearer. And I've been wasting away. No light in my eyes. Death is here, and I've been worrying about my gut. Worrying about getting my gut better, and this is death. Is it really death?'

Horror swept over him again, he gasped for breath, bent over and groped for the matches, leaning with one elbow on the bedside table. It was in his way, hurting him; he lost his temper with it, pressing down on it even harder in exasperation, and knocked it over. Breathless and in despair, he flopped down on to his back, expecting to die at any moment.

By this time the guests were leaving. Praskovya was seeing them out. She heard something fall, and came in.

'What's the matter?'

'Nothing. I just dropped something.'

She went out and came back with a candle. He lay there, puffing and panting heavily like a man who has just run a mile. His eyes settled on her.

'What's the matter, *Jean*?'

'No-thing. I . . . dropped it.' ('No use talking to her. She won't understand,' he thought.)

And she didn't. She picked up the candle and lit it for him, then she hurried out of the room to say goodnight to another guest.

When she came back he was still lying there on his back, staring upwards.

'What's wrong? Are you feeling worse?'

'Yes.'

She shook her head and sat down.

'Listen, *Jean*. I think perhaps we ought to ask Leshchetitsky to visit you at home.'

This meant asking the celebrated doctor to come to them, whatever the expense. He gave her a vitriolic smile and said no. She sat there for a while, then came over and kissed him on the forehead.

He hated her with every fibre of his being while she was kissing him, and it took all his strength not to push her away.

'Goodnight. God willing, you'll soon go to sleep.'

'Yes.'

6

Ivan Ilyich could see that he was dying, and he was in constant despair.

In the depths of his soul Ivan Ilyich knew he was dying but, not only could he not get used to the idea, he didn't understand it, couldn't understand it all.

All his life the syllogism he had learned from Kiesewetter's logic – Julius Caesar is a man, men are mortal, therefore Caesar is mortal – had always seemed to him to be true only when it applied to Caesar, certainly not to him. There was Caesar the man, and man in general, and it was fair enough for them, but he wasn't Caesar the man and he wasn't man in general, he had always been a special being, totally different from all others, he had been Vanya with his mama and his papa, with Vitya and Volodya, with his toys, and the carriage-driver, then little Katya, Vanya with all the delights, sorrows and rapture of childhood, boyhood and youth. Did Caesar have anything to do with the smell of that little striped leather ball that Vanya had loved so much? Was it Caesar who had kissed his mother's hand like that, and was it for Caesar that the silken folds of his mother's dress had rustled the way they did? Was he the one who had rebelled at law school over the provision of snacks? Had Caesar been in love like him? Could Caesar chair a session like him?

Yes, Caesar is mortal and it's all right for him to die, but not me, Vanya, Ivan Ilyich, with all my feelings and thoughts – it's different for me. It can't be me having to die. That would be too horrible.

These were the feelings that came to him.

'If I had to be like Caesar and die, I would have been aware of it, an inner voice would have told me, but there hasn't been anything like that on the inside. I've always thought – and all my friends have too – that we're not the same as Caesar. And now look what's happened!' he said to himself. 'It can't be. It can't be, but it is. How can it be? What's it all about?'

He couldn't understand, and he tried to banish the idea – it was false, wrong and morbid – and replace it with proper, healthy thinking. But the same thought – it wasn't just a thought but something that seemed like reality – kept coming back and facing him.

And in order to dispel these thoughts he started calling up different thoughts one after another, hoping to get support from them. He tried to get back to his earlier ways of thinking which had once protected him from thinking about death. But, strange to say, everything that once had protected him by hiding and eliminating any awareness of death was unable to perform that function now. In these latter days Ivan Ilyich spent most of his time trying to get back to the earlier ways of feeling that had protected him from death. He would say to himself, 'I must get down to some work. When all's said and done it's what I've been living for.' And he would go off to court banishing all his doubts, get into conversation with his colleagues and casually take his seat as he had done so many times before, contemplating the crowd before him with a pensive air and resting his wasted hands on the oaken arms of his chair, leaning over in his usual way to exchange whispered words with a colleague while toying with a file before raising his eyes suddenly and sitting up straight in order to go through the familiar words and begin the proceedings. But then suddenly there it was, the pain in his side, irrespective of where they had got to in the proceedings, and it was beginning to gnaw at him. Ivan Ilyich focused on it, drove the thought of it away, but it continued to make itself felt. *It* kept coming back, facing him and looking at him, while he sat there rigid, the fire went out of his eyes and he began to wonder whether *It* was the only truth. And his colleagues and subordinates looked on in distress, amazed that he, a man of such brilliant and subtle judgement, was getting confused and making mistakes. He would pull himself together, try to bring himself round and somehow bring the session to a conclusion, only to return home sadly aware that his judicial work could no longer hide him, as it once had done, from what he wanted to conceal, that he could not use his judicial work to rid himself of *It*. And the worst thing was that *It* was distracting him not in order to make him do something but only to get him to look *It* straight in the eye, just look at *It* and do nothing but suffer beyond words.

And in order to escape from this situation Ivan Ilyich sought other forms of consolation, other ways of screening it off; other screens appeared and for a while they seemed to be the saving of him, but immediately they were not so much destroyed as shone right through; it was as if *It* could penetrate anything, no defence being any good.

Sometimes in these latter days he would go into the drawing-room that he had furnished – the very room where he had had his fall, the room which (it was bitterly amusing to reflect) he had given his life to furnish, because he knew his illness had started with that bruise – he would go in and notice a scratch on a lacquered table top left behind by something sharp. Looking for the cause he would find it in the decorative bronze work on an album with one edge bent up. He would pick up the album, an expensive one which he had compiled with loving care, annoyed at the carelessness shown by his daughter and her friends – it was torn in places and some of the photographs were upside-down. He would go to a lot of trouble sorting it out and bending the bronze work back into place.

Then it would occur to him to move this entire

établissement of albums over into a corner near the flowers. He would call the footman. Either his wife or daughter would come to help. They wouldn't agree, they would take issue with him, he would argue and lose his temper – but none of this mattered because he had stopped remembering *It*. *It* was nowhere to be seen.

But once, when he was moving something himself, his wife said, 'Let the servants do that. You'll hurt yourself again,' and suddenly *It* flashed through the screen – he saw *It*. *It* flashed at him, and even as he longed for *It* to disappear he couldn't help focusing on his side – still there, the same ache that would not be ignored, and *It* was staring straight at him from behind the flowers. What was it all about?

'And that's the truth of it – I've lost my life here on this curtain, my battleground. Have I really? How horrible and how stupid! It can't be! It can't be, but it is.'

He would go into his study, lie down and find himself alone again with *It*. Face to face with *It*. Nothing to be done about *It*. Only stare at *It* and go cold.

7

How it came about in the third month of Ivan Ilyich's illness no one could have said, because it came on imperceptibly, by stages, but it happened that all of them, his wife, and daughter, and son, and the servant, and their friends, and the doctors, and most importantly he himself – everybody knew that the only interesting thing about him now was whether it would take him a long time to give up his place, finally release the living from the oppression caused by his presence, and himself be released from his suffering.

He slept less and less. He was given opium and injected with morphine, but this brought no relief. To begin with the dull feeling of anguish which he experienced in his semiconscious state gave him a sense of relief simply by being something new, but then it became just as agonizing as the raw pain, perhaps more so.

They gave him special food cooked from recipes provided by the doctors, but the food became more and more tasteless, more and more repulsive.

For the call of nature he also had special arrangements, and each time it was agonizing. The agony came from the dirtiness, the unseemliness, the smell and also the knowledge that someone else had to be involved in it.

But this most unpleasant business brought one consolation to Ivan Ilyich. The person who came to take things away was Gerasim, the peasant servant who waited on them at table.

Gerasim was a clean, fresh peasant lad, always bright and cheerful, who had fattened up on city food. To begin with Ivan Ilyich was embarrassed to watch him, always so neatly dressed in his Russian costume, performing such a distasteful service.

One day as he got up from the chamber pot not strong enough to pull up his own trousers he collapsed into a soft armchair and looked down in horror at his bared puny thighs with their starkly protruding muscles.

Who should come in but Gerasim, wearing his thick boots and exuding both their nice tarry smell and that of the fresh winter air, Gerasim with his light but firm tread, sporting a clean hessian apron and a clean cotton shirt, with his sleeves rolled up his bare strong young arms, and without a glance at Ivan Ilyich – to spare the sick man's feelings he was clearly suppressing the joyful vitality that shone from his face – he walked over to the pot.

'Gerasim,' said Ivan Ilyich feebly.

Gerasim started, clearly worried that he might have done something wrong, and in one swift movement he presented to the sick man his fresh, kind, open young face which was showing the first traces of a beard.

'Yes, sir?'

'This is not very nice for you, is it? You'll have to forgive me. I can't help it.'

'Please don't worry, sir.' And Gerasim's eyes flashed as he bared his young white teeth. 'It's no trouble. You're a sick man.'

And with his quick strong hands he did his usual thing and walked out with a light step. And five minutes later with the same light step he came back in.

Ivan Ilyich was still sitting there in his armchair.

'Gerasim,' he said, when the lad had replaced the clean, freshly washed chamber pot. 'Would you mind helping me? Over here.' Gerasim came across. 'Lift me up please. I can't manage it on my own, and I've sent Dmitriy away.'

Gerasim came over. In one movement that was as easy as his way of walking, he put his strong arms gently round Ivan Ilyich, lifted him up and held him with one hand, pulled up his trousers with the other, and tried to settle him down. But Ivan Ilyich asked to be taken across to the sofa. Effortlessly and apparently without tightening his grip, Gerasim took him, almost carried him, to the sofa and settled him down there.

'Thank you. You do everything so . . . nicely. So well.'

Gerasim gave another smile and made as if to leave the room. But Ivan Ilyich felt so comfortable with him that he didn't feel like letting him go.

'That's better . . . Would you mind moving that

chair over here? No, that one. Under my legs. It feels easier when my legs are up high.'

Gerasim brought the chair over, set it squarely on the floor without banging it down, and lifted Ivan Ilyich's legs up on to it. Ivan Ilyich felt an easing of the pain as Gerasim raised his legs.

'I feel better when my legs are up,' said Ivan Ilyich. 'Would you put that cushion under me?'

Gerasim did so. He raised his legs again and put the cushion under them. Again Ivan Ilyich felt better when Gerasim was holding his legs. When he lowered them he felt worse.

'Gerasim,' he asked. 'Are you busy just now?'

'Not in the slightest, sir,' said Gerasim, who had learned from the townspeople how to speak to the masters.

'What do you have on at the moment?'

'What do I have on? I've done everything there is to do – except chop the firewood for tomorrow.'

'Well, I'd like you to hold my legs up. Would you mind?'

'Of course not. I don't mind.' Gerasim held his legs up, and Ivan Ilyich could have sworn that in this position he couldn't feel any pain.

'But what about the firewood?'

'Don't you worry about that, sir. We'll manage.'

Ivan Ilyich told Gerasim to sit down and hold his legs up. He struck up a conversation, and, strangely enough, he seemed to feel better with Gerasim holding his legs.

After that Ivan Ilyich would send for Gerasim

now and then and have his legs held up on his shoulders. He liked it when they talked to each other. Gerasim did all of this easily, willingly and with a kindliness that Ivan Ilyich found moving. Health, strength and vitality in all other people were offensive to Ivan Ilyich; only Gerasim's strength and vitality gave him comfort rather than distressing him.

Ivan Ilyich's worst torment was the lying – the lie, which was somehow maintained by them all, that he wasn't dying, he was only ill, and all he had to do was keep calm and follow doctor's orders and then something good would emerge. Whereas he knew that whatever was done to him nothing would emerge but more and more agony, suffering and death. And this lie was torture for him – he was tortured by their unwillingness to acknowledge what they all knew and he knew; they wanted to lie to him about his terrible situation, and they wanted him – they were compelling him – to be a party to this lie. All this lying to him, lie upon lie, on the eve of his death, lying that was inexorably reducing the solemn act of his death to the same level as their social calls, their draperies, the sturgeon for dinner . . . it was all a terrible torment for Ivan Ilyich. And strangely enough, on many occasions when they were acting out this farce in front of him he was within a hair's breadth of screaming at them, 'Stop all this lying! You know and I know that I'm dying, so the least you can do is stop lying to me.' But he never quite had the nerve to do it. He could see that the awful, terrible act of his dying had been reduced by those around him to the level of an unpleasant incident, something rather indecent (as if they were dealing with someone who had come into the drawing-room and let off a bad smell), and this was done by exploiting the very sense of 'decency' that he had been observing all his life. He could see that no one had any pity for him because no one had the slightest desire to understand his situation. Gerasim was the only one who did understand his situation, and he was sorry for him. This was why Ivan Ilyich felt comfortable only with Gerasim. It was a comfort to him when Gerasim, sometimes for nights on end, held his legs up and refused to go to bed, saying, 'Please don't worry about it, Ivan Ilyich. I'll catch up on my sleep.' Or else he would suddenly address him in familiar language and add, 'It'd be different if you weren't ill, but with things the way they are why shouldn't I help you out?' Gerasim was the only one who didn't lie to him; everything showed that he was the only one who understood what was going on and saw no need to hide it. He just felt sorry for his weak and emaciated master. Once when Ivan Ilyich was dismissing him he put it quite bluntly: 'We've all got to die one day. Why shouldn't I give you a hand?' This was to say there was a good reason for not making a fuss about helping out: he was doing it for a dying man and he hoped that when his time came someone would help him out in the same way.

Apart from all this lying, or perhaps because of

it, the most tormenting thing of all for Ivan Ilyich was the fact that no one showed him any pity in the way that he wanted them to. There were some moments, after long periods of suffering, when what Ivan Ilyich wanted more than anything else – however embarrassed he would have been to admit it – what he wanted was for someone to take pity on him as if he were a sick child. He wanted to be kissed and cuddled and have a few tears shed over him in the way that children are cuddled and comforted. He knew he was a big man and something of a greybeard, which made this impossible, but nevertheless that is what he wanted. And his relationship with Gerasim offered something close to this, which was why the relationship with Gerasim gave him comfort.

Here is Ivan Ilyich wanting to weep, wanting to be cuddled and have tears shed over him, in comes his colleague Shebek, and instead of weeping and getting some tenderness Ivan Ilyich puts on a solemn and serious face, looks thoughtful and from sheer habit not only comments on the significance of a decision handed down by the Court of Cassation, but goes on to defend it strongly.

It was this living a lie, all around him and within him, that did most to poison the last days in the life of Ivan Ilyich.

8

It was morning. It was morning only because Gerasim had gone and Pyotr the servant was there, putting out the candles, opening one curtain and quietly tidying up. Morning or evening, Friday or Sunday – it didn't matter, it was all the same – grinding, agonizing pain, never for a moment relenting; an awareness of life hopelessly slipping away but not yet gone; the same terrible, relentless approach of hateful death, the only reality; and still all that lying. With all of this, what did the days, weeks and hours matter?

'Can I get you some tea, sir?'

'He likes good order. The masters must have their tea in the morning,' he thought, but all he said was, 'No.'

'Would you care to move over to the sofa, sir?'

'He wants to tidy the room, and I'm in the way. I am dirt and disorder,' he thought, but all he said was 'No. Leave me alone.'

The servant went about his work again. Ivan Ilyich stretched out one hand. Pyotr came over ready to help.

'What can I do for you, sir?'

'My watch.'

Pyotr took the watch, which was lying nearby, and handed it over.

'Half past eight. Are they still in bed?'

'No sir, they're not. Master Vasily [his son] has gone to school, and madam asked me to wake her if you wanted her. Shall I do that?'

'No. Don't bother.' Ivan Ilyich wondered whether to try some tea. Yes. 'Bring me some tea.'

Pyotr moved towards the door. Ivan Ilyich felt terrified at the thought of being left alone. How could he stop him leaving? Oh yes, medicine. 'Pyotr, would you give me my medicine?' Well, why not? The medicine might help. He took a spoonful and swallowed it. No, it wouldn't help. It was all rubbish. Just pretending. He felt sure of this as the old familiar taste returned, sickly and beyond hope. No, his faith was gone. And the pain, the pain, why couldn't it ease up just for a minute? He gave a groan. Pyotr came back in.

'No, carry on. Get me some tea.'

Pyotr left the room. Ivan Ilyich groaned, not really from the pain, however terrible that was, but from anguish. It was the same thing all the time, day and night with no end to it. Make it soon. Make *what* soon? Death, darkness. No, no. Anything was better than death!

When Pyotr came back in with the tea tray Ivan Ilyich looked at him distractedly for some time, unable to work out who he was or what he was doing there. Pyotr was embarrassed by the long look. The embarrassment brought Ivan Ilyich to his senses.

'Yes,' he said, 'Tea . . . Good. Leave it there. But I'd like you to help me get washed and put a clean shirt on.'

And Ivan Ilyich began to wash himself. With pauses for rest he washed his hands and face, cleaned his teeth, combed his hair and then took a look in the mirror. He was horrified. The most horrible thing was the limp way his hair stuck to his pallid forehead.

As he had his shirt changed he knew it would be more horrible still to glance down at his body, so he looked away. At last it was done. He put on his dressing-gown, wrapped a rug round himself and sat down in the armchair with his tea. For one moment he felt refreshed but at the first drink of tea there it was again, the same taste, the same pain. He forced the tea down, then lay back and stretched out his legs. He lay down and told Pyotr he could go.

The same thing again. One glittering drop of hope followed by a raging sea of despair, and nothing but pain, more pain, more anguish, always the same thing. It was depressing to be left alone, and he felt like calling somebody in, but he knew in advance that to have other people there would be even worse. Oh for another dose of morphine – he might lose himself in that. He must tell that doctor to think of something else. 'I can't go on like this. I can't.'

An hour goes by like this, then another. The bell rings in the hall – could it be the doctor? Yes, it is, the doctor, fresh and cheerful, fleshy and hearty, with a look on his face that seems to say well now, you seem to have had a bit of a fright, but we'll soon sort you out. The doctor knows that this look is out of place here, but he has assumed it once and for all and he can't get rid of it any more than a man who has gone out visiting can get rid of the frock-coat he put on that morning.

The doctor rubs his hands cheerfully, reassuringly.

'Chilly out there. Thick frost. Give me a minute to get warmed up.' His manner of speaking implies that he won't take long, he just needs to warm up and once he is warmed up he'll put everything right.

'Right then. How are you feeling?'

Ivan Ilyich senses that the doctor feels like saying, 'How's tricks?' but even he can see that this won't do, so he says,

'What sort of night did you have?'

Ivan Ilyich fixes the doctor with a look that seems to ask whether anything would ever make him feel too ashamed to go on lying. The doctor does not wish to understand.

So Ivan Ilyich says, 'No change. Terrible. The pain won't go. It's there all the time. There must be something you can do!'

'Yes, it's normal for patients like you to say that sort of thing. Right then. I think I'm warm enough now. Your good lady is a stickler for these things, but even she wouldn't say I was too cold. So. Good morning to you . . .' And the doctor shakes him by the hand.

And now, dropping all the banter, the doctor adopts a serious attitude and begins to examine the patient – pulse, temperature, tapping and listening.

Ivan Ilyich knows full well – it is beyond doubt – that this is all nonsense, an empty sham, but when the doctor goes down on his knees, reaches across him, applies his ear higher up and lower down, and then with the gravest look on his face performs a selection of gymnastic contortions Ivan Ilyich accedes to this just as he once acceded to speeches from lawyers even when he was well aware that they were lying, and why they were lying.

The doctor is still kneeling on the sofa, busily tapping away, when from the doorway comes the rustling of a silk dress and Praskovya can be heard reproaching Pyotr for not letting her know the doctor has arrived.

She comes in, kisses her husband and immediately begins to make it clear that she has been up for some time and only a little misunderstanding has prevented her from being there when the doctor arrived.

Ivan Ilyich looks at her searchingly, resenting everything about her, the whiteness, fullness and cleanliness of her arms and neck, the sheen of her hair and the light in her eyes that are so full of life. He loathes her with every fibre of his being.

Physical contact with her is agony for him because it brings on a surge of loathing.

Her attitude towards him and his illness is still the same. Just as the doctor has worked out an attitude towards his patients which he cannot now get rid of, she has worked out a particular attitude towards him – he is failing to do something he ought to do, and it's his fault, and she lovingly reproaches him for it – and she has not been able to rid herself of this attitude towards him.

'He just won't do as he's told! He forgets to take his medicine. And the worst thing is he will lie there in a position that must be bad for him – with his legs up.'

She described how he got Gerasim to hold his legs up for him.

The doctor gave a sweetly condescending smile. 'Can't be helped,' he seemed to be saying. 'These sick people do sometimes have silly ideas. We can't blame them.'

When the examination was over the doctor consulted his watch and then Praskovya informed Ivan Ilyich that, like it or not, she had invited a celebrated specialist to visit them that day and along with Mikhail Danilovich (the name of the regular doctor) he would conduct an examination and consultation.

'Now please don't argue with me. I'm doing this for myself,' she said sarcastically, implying that she was doing it all for him and this alone deprived him of any right to refuse. He scowled and said nothing. He felt that the lies that enveloped him were now so messy that he could hardly make sense of anything.

Everything she did for him she was doing for herself, and she told him she was doing for herself what she was actually doing for herself, but she made it sound so implausible that he was forced to assume the opposite.

Sure enough, at half past eleven the celebrated specialist arrived. More soundings and grave consultations both in his presence and in the next room concerning the kidney and the blind gut, with questions and answers expressed with such an air of gravity that, instead of the real life and death question which was the only one staring him in the face, up came the question of his kidney and blind gut, which were not doing quite what they should and which would shortly be set upon by Mikhail Danilovich and made to work properly.

The celebrated specialist took his leave looking serious but not hopeless. And in answer to the question put to him diffidently by Ivan Ilyich, whose eyes were glistening with fear and hope, as to whether there was any possibility of recovery, he replied that nothing could be guaranteed but there was a possibility. The look of hope on Ivan Ilyich's face as he watched the doctor leave was so pathetic that when she saw it Praskovya actually burst into tears as she walked out of the study to give the celebrated specialist his fee.

The lifting of his spirits induced by the doctor's

words of encouragement was short-lived. It was still the same room, the same pictures, curtains, wallpaper, medicine bottles, and the same body, his body, still suffering, racked with pain. And Ivan Ilyich began to moan, so they gave him an injection and he lapsed into unconsciousness.

When he came to, it was getting dark. They brought him his dinner. He forced down a little thin soup, then it was the same again, with another night coming on.

When dinner was over, at seven o'clock, Praskovya came in dressed for going out, with her ample breasts well supported and traces of powder on her face. That morning she had reminded him that they were going to the theatre. Sarah Bernhardt was in town, and they had a box which they had taken at his insistence. By now he had forgotten this, and he was offended to see her dressed up. But he hid his feelings when he remembered having insisted that they reserve the box and go, this being an aesthetic experience of educational value for the children.

As she came in Praskovya had looked pleased with herself, if rather guilty. She sat down on the edge of a chair and asked how he was feeling, though he could see that she was asking for the sake of asking rather than to find out, since she knew there was nothing to find out, and then she launched into what she felt she had to say, that nothing would have induced her to go out tonight, but the box had been reserved, Hélène and her daughter were going and so was Petrishchev (their daughter's fiancé, the examining magistrate), and they couldn't be allowed to go alone. But for that, she would have preferred to stay in with him. And he must be sure to follow the doctor's orders while she was out.

'Oh yes, and Fyodor [the fiancé] would like to come in. Do you mind? And Liza.'

'Let them come in.'

In came his daughter, dressed up to the nines, an exposed young body – while his body was causing him so much suffering. And she was flaunting it. Healthy and strong, obviously in love, she had no time for the illness, suffering and death that were marring her happiness.

In came Fyodor Petrovich, also in evening dress and sporting an *à la Capoul* hairstyle. The veins stood out on his long neck which was squeezed into its tight collar over a vast expanse of white shirt-front, and his narrow black trousers were tightly stretched over his strong thighs. One of his hands wore a close-fitting white glove and he carried an opera hat.

Creeping in unobtrusively behind him came the schoolboy, wearing a new uniform and gloves, poor chap, with terrible dark-blue rings under his eyes, the meaning of which was not lost on Ivan Ilyich.

He had always felt sorry for his son. And his frightened, compassionate look was dreadful to behold. Apart from Gerasim, Ivan Ilyich thought, Vasya was the only one who understood and felt sorry for him.

They all sat down and asked how he was feeling. Then for a while no one spoke. Liza asked her mother whether she had the opera glasses. Mother and daughter had a little argument about who had put them where. It ended nastily.

Fyodor asked Ivan Ilyich whether he had ever seen Sarah Bernhardt. At first Ivan Ilyich didn't quite catch what the question was, but then he said, 'No. Have you?'

'Yes. In *Adrienne Lecouvreur*.'

Praskovya mentioned something she had been particularly good in. Her daughter demurred. They were off into a conversation about her charm and naturalism as an actress, the same old conversation that everybody else has.

In the midst of it Fyodor looked across at Ivan Ilyich and suddenly broke off. The others looked, and they stopped too. Ivan Ilyich was staring straight ahead, his eyes glittering, and he was obviously furious with them. Things had to be put right, but there was absolutely no way of putting things right. Somehow the silence had to be broken. No one made a move, and everyone was becoming terrified that the living lie demanded by propriety would somehow be shattered and seen by everyone for what it was. It was Liza who made the first move. She broke the silence. She wanted to cover up what everyone was feeling, but by speaking out she revealed it.

'Oh well, if we're *going* it's time we got started,' she said, glancing at her watch, a present from her

84

father, and she smiled almost imperceptibly at her young man to convey something known only to the two of them as she got up, rustling her skirts.

They all got up, took their leave and drove off.

When they had gone Ivan Ilyich seemed to feel easier; the lie had gone, gone away with them – but the pain was still there. That same pain, that same feeling of dread made sure that nothing was harder, nothing easier. Everything was worse.

Once again the minutes passed one after another, then the hours one after another; it was always the same, endlessly, and the inevitable end itself was all the more horrible.

'Yes, send Gerasim in,' he said in reply to a question from Pyotr.

9

It was late at night when his wife returned. She tiptoed into the room, but he heard her; he opened his eyes and rapidly closed them again. She wanted to dismiss Gerasim and sit with him herself. He opened his eyes and said, 'No. You go.'

'Are you in a lot of pain?'

'It doesn't matter.'

'Take some opium.'

He consented, and drank some. She went away.

Until about three in the morning he was in a state of excruciating pain and delirium. He dreamed that somehow he was being forced, along with his pain, into the depths of a narrow black sack, being forced further and further in and not quite getting there. It was a harrowing, agonizing process. And he was scared, he wanted to get through and out, he was struggling, trying to help. Then suddenly he lost his hold and fell, and woke up. Gerasim was still there, sitting at the foot of the bed, dozing quietly, patiently. And he himself was lying there with his withered stockinged legs raised up on Gerasim's shoulders. The same candle was there, with its shade, and the same unremitting pain.

'Go away, Gerasim,' he whispered.

'I don't mind, sir. I'll just sit here for a bit longer.'

'No, you go away.'

He lowered his legs, turned sideways on to one arm and felt sorry for himself. He waited only for Gerasim to go out into the next room, and then he could restrain himself no longer: he burst into tears like a child. He was weeping because of his own helpless state, and his loneliness, and other people's cruelty, and God's cruelty, and God's non-existence.

'Why hast Thou done all of this? Why hast Thou brought me to this point? Why oh why dost Thou torture me like this . . . ?'

He was not expecting any answers; he was weeping because there were not and could not be any answers. The pain struck him again, but he didn't move and didn't call out. He said to himself, 'Here it comes again. Hit me then! But what's it for? What have I done to Thee? What is it for?'

Then he fell silent, and not only stopped crying, he stopped breathing. Suddenly he was all ears; he seemed to be listening not to a voice speaking in words but to the voice of his soul, the thoughts welling up in his mind.

'What do you want?' was the first expressible concept that came to him. 'What do you want? What do you want?' he repeated to himself. 'What is it?'

'No more pain. Staying alive,' came the answer.

And once again his concentration became so intense that not even the pain could distract him.

'Staying alive? How?' asked the voice of his soul.

'Oh, life like it used to be. Happy and good.'

'Life like it used to be? Happy and good?' came the voice.

And in his imagination he started to run through the best times of his happy life. But what was strange was that all the best times of his happy life no longer seemed anything like what they had been before. Nothing did – except the first recollections of his childhood. There, in his childhood, there was something truly happy that he could have lived with if it returned. But the person living out that happiness no longer existed; it was like remembering someone quite different.

At the point where he, today's Ivan Ilyich, began to emerge, all the pleasures that had seemed so real melted away now before his eyes and turned into something trivial and often disgusting.

And the further he was from childhood, the nearer he got to the present day, the more trivial and dubious his pleasures appeared. It started with law school. That had retained a little something that was still really good: there was fun, there was friendship, there was hope. But in the last years the good times had become more exceptional. Then, at the beginning of his service with the governor some good times came again: memories of making love to a woman. Then it became all confused, and the good times were not so many. After that there were fewer still; the further he went the fewer there were.

Marriage . . . an accident and such a disappointment, and his wife's bad breath, and all that sensuality and hypocrisy! And the deadliness of his working life, and those money worries, going on for a year, two years, ten, twenty – always the same old story. And the longer it went on the deadlier it became.

'It's as if I had been going downhill when I thought I was going uphill. That's how it was. In society's opinion I was heading uphill, but in equal measure life was slipping away from me . . . And now it's all over. Nothing left but to die!

'So what's it all about? What's it for? It's not possible. It's not possible that life could have been as senseless and sickening as this. And if it has really been as sickening and senseless as this why do I have to die, and die in agony? There's something wrong. Maybe I didn't live as I should have done?' came the sudden thought. 'But how can that be when I did everything properly?' he wondered, instantly dismissing as a total impossibility the one and only solution to the mystery of life and death.

'So, what *do* you want now? To live? Live how? To live as you do in court when the usher yells out, "The Court is in session!"' Court in session, sessions in court, he repeated to himself. 'Here comes judgement! But I'm not guilty,' he cried out angrily. 'What is this for?'

And he stopped crying, turned to face the wall and let his mind dwell on one single question: 'Why all this horror? What's the reason for it?'

But, for all his dwelling on it, he could find no answer. And whenever the thought occurred to him – which it often did – that all this was happening to him because he had been living the wrong kind of life, he would instantly remember how proper his life had been and dismiss such a bizarre notion.

IO

Another two weeks went by. Ivan Ilyich no longer rose from his sofa. He didn't care to lie in bed, so he lay on the sofa. And lying there, almost invariably facing the wall, he endured all the inexplicable agony in solitude, and in solitude he brooded on the same inexplicable question: 'What is this? Can it really be death?' And an inner voice would reply, 'Yes, that's what it is.' 'What is this torture for?' And the voice would reply, 'It's just there. It's not for anything.' Above and beyond this there was nothing.

From the very onset of his illness, since the first time he had driven round to see the doctor, his life had divided itself into two opposite and alternating moods: either despair and the anticipation of a horribly incomprehensible death or hope accompanied by a obsessive fascination for the workings of his body. He had eyes for only two things: either a kidney or blind gut that had temporarily stopped doing what it should do, or a horribly incomprehensible death, which there was no way to avoid.

These two moods alternated in him from the very outset of his illness, but the further the illness progressed the more dubious and preposterous his notions of a kidney became, and the more realistic was his awareness of impending death.

All he had to do was remember what he had been like three months before and what he was now, remember how steadily he had gone downhill, and any possibility of hope was shattered.

In his last days of solitude, when he found himself lying there facing the back of the sofa, solitude in the midst of a populous city and his own friends and family – a solitude more complete than anything anywhere, at the bottom of the sea or in the bowels of the earth – in these last days of terrible solitude Ivan Ilyich lived only by recreating the past. Images of his past life came back to him one after another. This process always began with the most recent ones and proceeded back to the most remote, to childhood, and there it lingered. If Ivan Ilyich remembered the stewed prunes he had been offered for dinner that day he would remember the raw and wrinkly French prunes of his childhood, their special taste and how his mouth watered when he got down to the stone, and along with the memory of that taste would come a whole series of further memories of that time: his nurse, his brother, his toys. 'No don't, not that. It's too painful,' Ivan Ilyich would say to himself, transporting himself back to the present: there it was – a button of the back of the sofa, creases in the morocco. 'Morocco is expensive, and it doesn't wear well. It started an argument. But that was different morocco and a different argument – when we tore father's briefcase and got punished, and mother brought us some tarts.' Once again his thoughts were settling on his childhood, and again they were too painful for Ivan Ilyich, so he tried to drive them away and think of something else.

And once again, along with this train of recollections, another train of recollections troubled his spirit – the way in which his illness had grown and got worse. Here too, the further back he went the more life there was. More goodness in life, more of life itself. The two things were merging. 'It's like the pain getting worse and worse – all of my life has been getting worse and worse,' he thought. There was one point of light back there at the beginning of life, but after that everything had been getting blacker and blacker. 'In inverse proportion to the square of the distance from death,' he thought. And this image of a stone accelerating as it flies down imprinted itself on his soul. Life, a series of increasing sufferings, flies ever faster towards its end, the most terrible suffering. 'I'm flying somewhere . . .' He would shiver and shudder, trying to resist, but he knew by now that resistance was impossible, and he would turn his eyes to the back of the sofa, eyes that were weary of looking, but couldn't stop looking, at what lay ahead. And he was waiting, waiting for that terrible fall, shock and annihilation. 'Resistance is impossible,' he would say to himself, 'but if only I could see what it's all about! No, that's impossible too. There would be an explanation if I could say I've been wrong in the way I've lived my life. But you couldn't say that. It's not possible,' he would tell himself, recalling how fastidious he had been about the propriety and respectability of his life. 'You can't say that. It's not possible,' he would tell himself, twisting his lips into a smile as if someone might see it and be taken in by it. 'There is no explanation. Agony and death . . . What for?'

II

Two weeks went by like this. During those two weeks an event took place that Ivan Ilyich and his wife had been hoping for: Petrishchev made a formal proposal. It happened one evening. The next morning Praskovya came in to see her husband, wondering how best to break the news of Fyodor's proposal, but during that night Ivan Ilyich's condition had taken another turn for the worse. Praskovya found him on the same sofa, but in a different position. He was lying flat on his back, moaning and staring ahead with a fixed look.

She started talking about his medicine. He transferred his gaze to her. She didn't finish what she had started to say; there was so much enmity in that gaze, and it was levelled straight at her.

'For Christ's sake, let me die in peace!' he said.

She made as if to leave the room, but at that moment in walked their daughter, who came over to say good morning. He gave her the same look he had directed at his wife, and in response to her inquiries about his health he said drily that soon he would no longer be a burden to them. Both of them sat on for a while, saying nothing, and then they left.

'What have we done wrong?' Liza asked her

mother. 'Anyone would think it was our fault. I'm sorry for papa, but why do we have to suffer?'

The doctor arrived at his usual time. Ivan Ilyich responded to him with a yes and no, fixing him with a malevolent look, and finally he said, 'Look, you know you can't help me. Just leave me alone.'

'We can ease the pain,' said the doctor.

'You can't. Leave me alone.'

The doctor went out into the drawing-room and told Praskovya that things were very bad. Only one thing could help – opium. That might ease the pain, which must be dreadful.

The doctor said that the physical pain must be dreadful, which was true. But more dreadful than the physical pain was the suffering in spirit, his greatest agony.

His spiritual suffering took the form of a thought that had suddenly struck him that night as he looked at Gerasim's sleepy-eyed, good-natured face with its high cheek bones. 'What if I really have been *wrong* in the way I've lived my whole life, my conscious life?'

It occurred to him that what had once seemed a total impossibility – that he had not lived his life as he should have done – might actually be true. It occurred to him that the slight stirrings of doubt he had experienced about what was considered good by those in the highest positions, slight stirrings that he had immediately repudiated – that these misgivings might have been true and everything else might have been wrong. His career, the ordering of his life, his family, the things that preoccupied people in society and at work – all of this might have been wrong. He made an attempt at defending these things for himself. And suddenly he sensed the feebleness of what he was defending. There was nothing to defend.

'But if it's like that,' he said to himself, 'and I am leaving this life knowing I have ruined everything I was given, and it can't be put right, what then?' He lay on his back and started to go through his whole life again in a different way. Next morning, when he saw his servant, then his wife, then his daughter, then the doctor – their every movement and every word bore out the terrible truth that had been revealed to him during the night. In them he saw himself and all he had lived by, and he could clearly see that it was all wrong; it was all a gross deception obscuring life and death. This knowledge exacerbated his physical suffering, making it ten times worse. He moaned and writhed, and clutched at his clothing, which seemed to be choking and stifling him. And he hated them for it.

After being given a heavy dose of opium he lost consciousness, but by dinner time it had all begun again. He sent everyone away, and lay there tossing and turning.

His wife came to him, and said, '*Jean*, darling, please do this for my sake.' (For *her* sake?) 'It can't do any harm, and it often helps. Look, it's nothing much. Even healthy people . . .'

He opened his eyes wide.

'What? Take communion? What for? I'm not doing that . . . Oh, I don't know . . .'

She burst into tears.

'All right, my dear? I'll send for our priest. He's such a nice man.'

'All right. That's fine,' he said.

When the priest came and heard his confession, Ivan Ilyich relaxed, feeling some relief from his doubts and therefore from his suffering, and he experienced a moment of hope. His mind turned again to his blind gut and the possibility of a cure for it. When he took communion there were tears in his eyes.

When he was laid down after taking communion he felt better for a while; there was hope that he might live on. His thoughts turned to the operation that he had been offered. 'I want to live. I do want to live,' he said to himself. His wife came in to greet him after communion. She said the usual things, and then added:

'You really do feel better, don't you?'

'Yes,' he said, looking away.

Her clothes, her figure, the look on her face, the sound of her voice – all said the same thing to him: 'This is wrong. Everything you have lived by, and still do, is a lie, a deception that hides life and death away from you.' And the moment this thought occurred to him, his hatred welled up, and along with the hatred came physical suffering and agony, and along with the agony came awareness of the inevitable destruction that was now so close. There was something different about it: a twisting, shooting pain, and constricted breathing.

The look on his face as he said 'Yes' had been dreadful. When he had got the word out, looking straight at her, he wrenched himself over face down remarkably quickly for one so weak, and roared at her:

'Get out! Go away! Leave me alone!'

12

From that moment on the screaming began. It went on unbroken for three days, so terrible that people two rooms away were horrified to hear it. At the moment when he had answered his wife he had realized he was done for, there was no way back, the end was here, the absolute end, and his unresolved doubts would remain as doubts.

'Oh! Oh! Oh!' he cried, varying the tone. He began by crying out, 'Oh no!' and went on screaming the letter 'o'. Throughout the three days, during which time had ceased to exist for him, he struggled with the black sack into which he was being crammed by an invisible, unstoppable force. He resisted like a condemned man resisting his executioner, knowing that he is not going to be spared, and with every minute that passed he sensed that despite all his fighting and struggling he was getting nearer and nearer to the thing that terrified him. He sensed that the pain came from being thrust into that black hole and, what was worse, not being able to get through. What was preventing him from getting through was his insistence that his life had been a good one. This vindication of his lifestyle was holding him down, preventing him from moving on, and causing him the greatest suffering.

Suddenly he felt a strong jolt in his chest and side, and a further constriction of his breathing. He was into the hole, and there at the end of the hole a kind of light was shining. What was happening to him was like when he had been in a railway carriage and you think you are going forwards but you are really going backwards, and suddenly you know what the right direction is.

'Yes, it's all been wrong,' he told himself, 'but that doesn't matter. It's possible to do the right thing. But what is the right thing?' he wondered, and suddenly he was calm.

It was nearing the end of the third day, an hour before his death. At that very moment his schoolboy son crept in to see his father, and came over to his bed. The dying man was still screaming desperately and waving his arms about. His hand happened to catch the boy's head. The boy took hold of it, pressed it to his lips and burst into tears.

This was the very moment when Ivan Ilyich had fallen through and seen a light, and it was revealed to him that his life had not been what it should have been, but that it could still be put right. He was wondering what the right thing was, and he had calmed down, listening. Now he could feel someone kissing his hand. He opened his eyes and looked at his son. He felt sorry for him. His wife came over. He looked at her. With her mouth open and the tears not wiped away from her nose and cheek she was looking at him in despair. He felt sorry for her.

'Yes, I'm hurting them,' he thought. 'They feel sorry for me, but they'll be all right when I'm dead.' He wanted to tell them this, but he wasn't strong enough to get the words out. 'Anyway . . . no good talking. Must *do* something.' He looked at his wife, motioned to their son and said:

'Take him away . . . sorry for him . . . and you . . .' He tried to say, 'Forgive me', but it came out as 'For goodness . . .' Too weak to correct himself, he waved his hand knowing that he who needed to would understand.

And suddenly everything was clear to him: what had been oppressing him and would not go away *was* now going away, all at once, on two sides, ten sides, all sides.

He felt sorry for them, and he must do something to stop hurting them. Set them free, and free himself from all this suffering. 'So nice, and so simple,' he thought. 'But what about the pain?' he wondered. 'Where's it gone? Hey, pain, where are you?'

He listened and waited.

'Oh, here it comes. So what? Bring on the pain.'

'What about death? Where is it?'

He was looking for his earlier, accustomed fear of death, but he couldn't find it. Where was death? What death? There was no fear whatsoever, because there was no death.

Instead of death there was light.

'So that's it!' he said suddenly, out loud. 'Oh, bliss!'

All of this happened to him in a single moment, and the meaning of that moment was not going to change. For those present his agony went on for another two hours. There was a rattling in his chest. His wasted body shook. Then the rattling and the wheezing dwindled away.

'He's gone!' said someone over him.

He caught these words and repeated them in spirit. 'Death has gone,' he told himself. 'It's gone.'

He took in some air, stopped halfway through a deep breath, stretched out, and died.

PENGUIN RED CLASSICS

MOZART'S JOURNEY TO PRAGUE
EDUARD MÖRIKE

Mozart is creative, brilliant and charming. But is he also a thief?

Making his way to Prague for the opening of *Don Giovanni*, the great composer playfully tries to steal an orange from a Bohemian family's garden. But no sooner has he taken the fruit than he is caught by a furious gardener. Desperate to escape, Mozart frantically scrawls an apologetic note to the owners of the tree.

Soon, he finds himself not only forgiven but welcomed by a family who have adored the beauty of his music and are stunned to find the celebrity wandering lost in their orangery. And when they reveal it is their daughter's wedding, there can only be one guest of honour: the musical genius Amadeus.

For classic fiction, read Red

www.penguinclassics.com/reds

PENGUIN RED CLASSICS

THE SORROWS OF YOUNG WERTHER
JOHANN WOLFGANG VON GOETHE

'Masterly and devastating' *Guardian*

You only find true love once.

When Werther dances with the beautiful Lotte, it seems as though he is in paradise. It is a joy, however, that can only ever be short-lived. Engaged to another man, she tolerates Werther's adoration and encourages his friendship. She can never return his love.

Broken-hearted, he leaves her home in the country, trying to escape his own desire. But when he receives a letter telling him that she is finally married, his passion soon turns to destructive obsession.

And as his life falls apart, Werther is haunted by one certainty:

He has lost his reason for living.

For classic fiction, read Red

www.penguinclassics.com/reds